SPECIAL MESSAGE TO READERS

THE ULVERSCROFT FOUNDATION
(registered UK charity number 264873)
was established in 1972 to provide funds for
research, diagnosis and treatment of eye diseases.
Examples of major projects funded by
the Ulverscroft Foundation are:-

- The Children's Eye Unit at Moorfields Eye Hospital, London
- The Ulverscroft Children's Eye Unit at Great Ormond Street Hospital for Sick Children
- Funding research into eye diseases and treatment at the Department of Ophthalmology, University of Leicester
- The Ulverscroft Vision Research Group, Institute of Child Health
- Twin operating theatres at the Western Ophthalmic Hospital, London
- The Chair of Ophthalmology at the Royal Australian College of Ophthalmologists

You can help further the work of the Foundation
by making a donation or leaving a legacy.
Every contribution is gratefully received. If you
would like to help support the Foundation or
require further information, please contact:

THE ULVERSCROFT FOUNDATION
The Green, Bradgate Road, Anstey
Leicester LE7 7FU, England
Tel: (0116) 236 4325
website: www.foundation.ulverscroft.com

SHADOW OF DOUBT

A local woman suddenly takes on a new identity and goes on the run to another town. Meanwhile, Cathcart's respected district attorney, Turner Redland, is being threatened with blackmail for no discernible reason. Defense attorney Gail Brevard and her husband and law partner, Conrad Osterwitz, are drawn into the net. When a local con artist and possible witness turns up dead, there are plenty of suspects for the crime. Will Gail be able to make sense of it all in order to save the innocent and bring the guilty to justice?

MARY WICKIZER BURGESS

♦

SHADOW OF DOUBT

A Gail Brevard murder mystery

Complete and Unabridged

LINFORD
Leicester

First published in Great Britain

First Linford Edition
published 2020

A catalogue record for this book is available
from the British Library.

ISBN 978–1–4448–4402–3

Published by
F. A. Thorpe (Publishing)
Anstey, Leicestershire

Set by Words & Graphics Ltd.
Anstey, Leicestershire
Printed and bound in Great Britain by
T. J. International Ltd., Padstow, Cornwall

This book is printed on acid-free paper

To Michael, as always . . .

1

It was snowing.

She turned and looked back at the way she had come. Dark gashes in the white counterpane betrayed her footsteps.

She shifted the pack on her shoulders and started in again, trudging towards the northwest, as nearly as she could judge. She should be nearing the old two-lane state highway soon. On the other side, she knew, cleared farmlands stretched for miles into the distance. There she might find a deserted barn or outbuilding where she could rest for the night.

She was counting on that.

Heavy wet flakes fell steadily from the sickly pale yellow sky. Soon her footsteps would be obliterated — and there would be no further evidence anyone had come this way at all.

* * *

Hours earlier, he had entered the back door and slammed it shut behind him, throwing his coat on the floor.

'Damn them,' he muttered under his breath. 'Damn them all to hell!'

'What's wrong?' She watched him nervously from the kitchen where she had begun to scrub the potatoes for dinner. Usually, he was in and settled by the time she came home from work. She could tell that today had been different and something wasn't right in his world.

'Shut up,' he threw at her. 'You don't know nothin' 'bout nothin.''

She started to reply, then snapped her mouth shut. It never did any good to try to reason with him . . . especially when he was in this mood.

He pulled out a half-full whiskey bottle and poured some into the smeared water glass he kept on the scarred table he called his desk. As many times as she had tried to clean off the space, he had just as often yelled and even thrown something at her for daring to touch his things.

He sat down and began rummaging through a sheaf of papers. She kept at her work, watching him surreptitiously. Whenever he began drinking like this, she needed to keep her guard up.

She put the potatoes on to boil and opened the oven to check the little roast inside. Maybe tonight was the night, she thought. Maybe it was time.

An hour later, she made her way across to the old tool shed on the other side of the yard. She stepped inside, savoring the odor of ancient machine oil. Waning sunlight drifted in from chinks in the dark wooden walls and ceiling. A sturdy, long-unused work bench was fastened along one wall, and rusting implements hung from hooks on the other side of the room. She did not know the purposes of most of them, but thought they looked as if they could be used for torturing or even killing something.

Shuddering, she moved past the tools to the back wall and pushed a single sliding door aside. This nook had an entirely different feel to it. Over time, she had laboriously whitewashed the walls, and one old glass pane window had been scrubbed clean to let in the light. A threadbare piece of fake oriental carpeting stretched over the floor. In one corner, an overstuffed chair she had found alongside the road sat, covered with a ragged quilt. A rickety table held writing instruments, and an easel near the window displayed an unfinished watercolor — a still life of flowers in a favorite vase.

This tiny room had been her safe haven. He never came in here and, indeed, had scoffed at her efforts to create this space of her own. Now she was ready to say goodbye to it all.

She would not miss any of it.

★   ★   ★

As she trudged forward through the brush and bare pines and scrub oak, all she could think of was getting away.

She didn't care where she ended up, so long as he — the monster — was no longer part of her life.

At last she broke through to the highway. It seemed deserted, but she held back behind the last of the straggling trees and waited a bit to catch her breath.

Fields of barley and oat stubble stretched as far as one could see along the other side of the winding road. Harvest had come and gone. All the hay and straw had been gleaned and baled and was now stored up in barns and sheds across the countryside. As the winter progressed, it would provide feed for all the stock which had not been butchered earlier in the year.

She raked her eyes across the landscape until she found what she needed — a lone storage shed of sorts, sticking out like a sore thumb. It did not seem too far from the roadside. But that didn't matter. It was probably her best bet for shelter before nightfall.

Looking up and down the highway, she took her chance and scooted across to the other side. Bending down the flimsy barbed wire, she stepped over and through, careful not to snag her clothing, and struck out across the field toward the building.

It was further than she thought, and she began to wonder if she would make it.

She kept to it, though, and eventually found herself in front of the ramshackle structure. It could hardly be called a building, it was so rundown. If only, she hoped, the sliding barn door was not padlocked. She had a couple of small tools in her pack, but they might not be strong enough to pry open a sturdy lock.

She was overjoyed to see that the door was securely hasped, but there was no lock on it. She easily slipped up the hasp and pushed the door aside just far enough to step inside. It was almost too dark to see, but she was prepared for that. At the end of a lanyard around her neck was a small but strong flashlight. She turned it on and looked about.

It wasn't a large structure, and it was filled nearly to capacity with stacked bales of freshly mown hay. Toward the back she could see loose straw piled up in what appeared to be a small stall or enclosure which might be used to house an injured or ill animal. In any case, it would make a suitable place to sleep, and she moved gratefully into the snug space, dropped her pack, and fell into the straw as if it were the most comfortable feather bed in the world.

But it was difficult to fall asleep. Her mind kept whirling as she reviewed the earlier events of the day.

Was she making the biggest mistake of her life?

No, she decided. Things had gone too far off the rails for that. There was no salvaging anything of value from that relationship. All she really felt was relief.

The nightmare was over. Now she must face reality.

⋆   ⋆   ⋆

She slept better than she thought she would.

Shafts of light began creeping in through the cracks in the walls. It was quiet, indicating that the storm of the night before had passed. She lay there a moment, wishing she could stay there in the warm straw. But she knew that was impossible. She had a lot of ground to cover today.

She felt about in her pack and pulled

out the wig. It was pageboy style in a warm reddish-brown, a little darker than her natural shade. She fitted it to her head the way the saleslady had showed her, and pulled her knitted cap on top to secure it.

Glancing in her compact, she quickly applied foundation, also in a darker shade, and deep red lipstick. The face peering back at her looked the same, yet different somehow.

Suddenly, a loud noise erupted outside the shed. She grabbed everything and dove back into the stall, backing up in a corner and pulling straw around and over her as best she could.

'That's got it,' came a man's shout. 'Stop right there.'

'Okay, Jesse,' was the response. 'Let's get 'er done. Those Betsys will be lookin' for their eats.'

With a bang, the barn door slid open and two middle-aged men in farm attire strode into the shed. Working quickly, they snagged up bales with vicious-looking hay hooks and grappled them out and onto a hauler attached to a big green

John Deere tractor.

'That's enough,' said Jesse. 'Don't want to make sissies of 'em. It's liable to be a long winter.'

'Okay,' responded his helper. 'Let's go.'

The door was slammed back into place, the tractor roared, and a few minutes later the noisy apparatus disappeared into the distance.

She waited a little while in stunned silence, wondering if the men would be far enough away to allow her to slip away unnoticed. Finally, she got up, brushed off as much of the straw as possible, shouldered the pack and made her way to the door. She shoved it, but was startled when nothing moved.

No! The farmers had secured the hasp from the outside when they closed the door.

She was trapped!

It was pretty stupid of her, not to think of that possibility. If she couldn't get out of the shed, she would be stuck here in limbo until Jesse and his pal came back again — and that might be a very long time; not until the next storm, she assumed. She could be dead by then!

She stopped, calmed herself and thought hard. All of her plans could come to nothing because of this one idiotic mistake. She could not allow that to happen.

She jiggled the door a bit to see if the hasp might fall away on its own. When that didn't work, she bent down and peered through the crack between the door and the frame.

She could see daylight! And she could also see the hasp itself clearly, securing the door. Quickly, she dug down into her pack and pulled out a small leather bag. She unzipped it and placed her fingers around the handle of a slim screwdriver. Carefully aiming it at the silvery metal of the hasp, she struck.

At first nothing happened. But the second time she hit it, the hasp burst free.

Once more she gathered up her belongings, shoved the door aside just enough to allow her to exit, and pulled it back again, securing it once more with the hasp.

Blowing her breath out in relief, she

looked up at the roadway across the field. Her research had confirmed that intra-state buses crisscrossed this route frequently, ferrying the locals from the many little towns scattered between here and the western and northern parts of the state. With any luck, she would be able to flag one down.

She knew the drivers would only take the exact amount of the fare. But she had recently purchased an intra-state bus pass, and if that didn't work, she also had coins and bills of various denominations.

Hopefully, one of those options would get her on to the next town. At least that was her plan.

★ ★ ★

She made her way down the tarmac highway as quickly as she could manage, the backpack bouncing against her shoulders. She was stiff and sore from the previous day's exertions, but tried to keep up a reasonable pace.

Finally, in half an hour or so, she reached an intersection of sorts. It was really only a dirt farm road that came up to and halted at the very edge of the crossroads. But, she reasoned, people from that farm might find it necessary to take the bus into town from time to time. And she was banking on that.

She stood there, looking about at the desolate landscape. The whole thing reminded her of the scene in Hitchcock's *North by Northwest*, when Cary Grant was chased around a cornfield by a crop duster. She half expected a nondescript car to drive up the dirt road and deposit an elderly man dressed in a dark suit. He would then stand and wait for the bus with her. But, of course, that didn't happen.

At last, just as she was beginning to give up hope, she heard first then spied a big grey bus with a bright red, white and blue logo on the side, trundling up the road towards her. She waved her hand at the driver, and he obligingly pulled over and levered the door to its open position.

'Where you headed, ma'am?' he called out politely.

'Newton. Are you going that far?'

12

'Yes. But we'll be making a half-hour rest stop on the way. We won't get into Newton, I reckon, before 4:00 p.m.'

'That's fine. I have an intra-state pass. But I also have change if that would work better for you.'

'Let's see the pass.' He scanned it quickly. 'Yes, that'll work. Do you want a return ticket?'

'No; I'm visiting a sick relative. I don't know how long I'll need to stay there.'

He nodded, clipped her pass, and handed her a stub. 'You'll need that to get back on if you get off at the rest stop.'

'Thanks,' she said, stuffing the ticket down into a zipper pocket in the pack.

She made her way down the aisle to an empty row, moved in and tucked her pack in between the innermost seat and the window, giving her a cushion of sorts to lean against while also protecting her possessions from being pilfered by curious passengers.

The door wheezed shut, and the big bus shifted back into gear and continued lumbering on down the road.

She cuddled up next to her pack and

let her mind wander. Eventually, she fell into a fitful doze, picturing a desperate Cary Grant running away from the crop duster.

He had escaped. She hoped she would be as lucky.

2

The intercom squawked, startling Gail out of her reverie.

'Ms. Brevard? I'm sorry but . . . wait. You can't . . . '

The office door opened and she found herself staring into the grinning face of Turner Redland. Her aide, Margaret, was standing behind him, anxiously wringing her hands.

'It's all right, Margaret. I'll see him.'

The older woman closed the door and scurried back down the hall to the safety of the reception area.

'Come in, Mr. District Attorney,' Gail said. 'This *is* a momentous occasion!'

Attorney Gail Brevard and D.A. Turner Redland had known each other since their law school days, and had even dated briefly in earlier years. But more often than not, they had been adversaries in the courtroom. And, she reflected with satisfaction, more often than not, she had been on the winning side.

'No reason to be so formal, Gail,' Turner said, taking a seat in front of her desk. 'How are things going for the firm? Pretty good, I imagine, since that spectacular victory in the Del Monaco trial. By the way, you and Connie — ' He was speaking of her husband and law partner, Conrad Osterlitz. ' — did a tremendous job with that case . . . not to mention allowing us to remove some really bad actors from the community.'

'Thanks.' She paused. 'Connie and I have reservations for dinner this evening, for the first time in quite a while. In fact, I'm expecting him to walk in the door any minute. Is there anything in particular you wanted to discuss?'

'Sorry; this won't take long.'

He reached down into his briefcase, a stunningly crafted affair constructed of shiny black alligator skin and some other type of leather. It probably had cost the lives of several endangered species.

'I'd like you to take a look at this,' he said, plonking a manila folder down in front of her. 'I think I might need my own counsel. And I'd like that to be you . . . if you're willing.'

She sat there, stunned. 'You've got to be kidding, Turner,' she said. 'You have a regular phalanx of very competent attorneys working for you already. Why on earth would you need me?'

'Well, that's just it, Gail. They all work for me as the D.A. I need someone independent and not part of the county bureaucracy. Just take a look at this. I think I'm being threatened — with blackmail, or whatever. By the way, do you remember Sam Weems?' he added, almost as an afterthought.

'Sam? Of course I remember him. I met him years ago, during the first Powell trial.'

She was puzzled. Sam Weems had been an investigative reporter assigned to the courthouse beat back in those days. He had risen in the world since, and was now managing editor of the local newspaper, *The Cathcart Daily Sun*. 'What's Sam Weems got to do with this?'

'There's a letter in this file from Sam which I think you might find of interest.

17

He's requesting an interview with me to 'answer allegations of misconduct' in the district attorney's office.'

Gail was silent for a moment. 'Have you seen or talked to him about the nature of the allegations?'

'No, I haven't. Frankly, I wasn't sure *what* I should do. I have no idea what he's talking about, Gail. And I sure as hell don't want to go in there and get blindsided with something.'

'Hmm. Give me a dollar,' Gail said.

Redland laughed. 'Good old Gail! You've never forgotten that cautionary advice from law school, have you? Sure, I'll hire you . . . for a buck's worth.' So saying, he pulled a dollar bill out of his wallet and handed it across the desk.

Gail wrote out a brief receipt on a notepad with her name engraved at the top and handed it to him. 'All right,' she said, 'now you have attorney-client privilege with me. We're safe as houses.'

Turner chuckled. 'Okay, Gail. Give me a dollar's worth of advice.'

'Let me put Hugo on it,' she said. 'Connie and I will look through your file

18

and see if anything seems particularly unusual or out of place. Would you mind talking to him at some point — Hugo, I mean — and answering a few questions or giving him your own guesses on this issue?'

Hugo Goldthwaite ran a private detective agency out of a suite of offices right down the hall from Gail and Connie's law firm. He was on permanent retainer with the firm. But beyond that fact, they all had been good friends for quite a few years. Hugo had even saved her life on at least one occasion, of that she was sure.

'Of course I don't mind,' Turner said. 'Bring Hugo in on this if you think he can help.'

'Good.' She looked up as the hall door opened again. 'Hi, Connie,' she said. 'Look who's paying us a visit.'

Conrad Osterwitz entered his wife's office and stared quizzically at the man seated across the desk from her. 'Well,' he said finally, 'this *is* a surprise. You slumming, Turner?'

'Hi, Connie,' Turner said. 'Long time, no see. Gail has already explained that you two have plans for tonight, so I won't take up any more of your time right now. Gail can explain everything to you. I want your take on this also.'

He stood, offered his hand to Connie, and nodded at Gail.

'By the way, I also wanted to give you my condolences on your loss, Gail. She was a fine human being and she'll be missed in the community.'

'Thank you,' Gail said. She looked down at the desk with glistening eyes.

'And extend that thought to Miss Lucy and your brother, as well. Here, let me give you this,' he added.

He pulled out a business card and wrote something on the back.

'That's my private number,' he said, handing it to her. 'Please give it to Miss Lucy and tell her if she has any concerns about anything at all, she should give me a call and I'll provide her any assistance she needs. That place is pretty isolated out there.'

'Why, thank you, Turner,' Gail said, taking the card from him. 'You know, Connie and I are planning to move in there just as soon as we can get some things done to the house. But I appreciate your thoughtfulness, and I'm sure Lucy will, too.'

Gail's mother had passed a few months earlier. Her cousin Lucy, a retired nurse, had been living in the old Norris home, helping to care for Gail's brother with special needs, Erle.

'And let me know as soon as you can what you decide about my dilemma,' he added. 'I really would appreciate any help or advice you could provide.' And with that, Turner Redland left the room.

'And, I suppose this is another fine mess? Connie said as he helped Gail on with her coat. 'What next?'

3

August had been an interesting month. The Del Monaco trial and its aftermath had taken up a good part of it for the firm, including a runaway witness, a gruesome murder, and an unexpected kidnapping. Somehow, Gail and her colleagues had weathered all the difficulties and had come out on top with the most lucrative win of their careers.

Immediately following the general office celebration and wrapping up of details, Connie had taken Gail aside.

'I've got something to say, Gail, and I want you to hear me out before you respond.'

He was serious, she realized, and she sat down across from him at the conference table and gave him her full attention.

'All right, I'm listening,' she said. 'What's wrong?'

'Nothing's wrong. Everything is *very* all

right.' He paused and smiled at her. 'I'm just going to ask you to marry me again — but this time I'm very serious about it, and I want you to consider what I'm about to say.'

She didn't respond at first. They had had this conversation several times. She had been married before, and it had not ended well. She was a great believer in the saying, 'If it ain't broke, don't fix it.' Most of all, she and Connie had a great relationship. She wasn't at all sure that marriage would be an improvement.

He continued: 'We've just had a very successful outcome to a very difficult case. The monetary benefit is going to be significant. I understand that we have all sorts of contracts and agreements between us to cover all kinds of situations, both legal and otherwise. And I'm comfortable with that.'

'But . . . ?'

'But there's one thing I *am* missing. I don't have any immediate family. As you know, I lost my parents at an early age, and I was an only child. I have no other close relatives. You and your family have become my family, too. I love your mom, your brother Erle, and cousin Lucy, just as if they were my own kin.

'My one nightmare is that something will happen to one of you and I won't be able to help or have a say in the matter because I'm not related in any way. If we were married, they'd become my next of kin, too. I'd feel as if I had more control, more *responsibility* towards all of you.

'Right now, I sometimes feel as if I'm a fifth wheel. It both annoys me and frightens me. I *want* to be a part of you and your family, legally, and in every other way. If something happened to *you*, God forbid, I want to be able to continue to care for them as if they were my own flesh and blood.

'And now that we've had this great financial plum fall in our laps, I feel like there's no good reason to hold us back any longer. That's all I have to say.'

He sat back and waited for her response without much hope in his eyes.

She looked at him. Here was the love of her life. They had been together for a number of years now. He had proven himself over and over to her. She knew beyond any shadow of doubt that he cared for her and would never let her down. What the hell was she waiting for?

'All right,' she said. 'But I don't want a big wedding. I don't think it would be appropriate. Just Mother, Erle, and Lucy should be there. What do you think?'

The smile he flashed startled her. Connie was pragmatic and down to earth. He rarely showed his emotions. But this was different.

'Thank you,' he said. But the kiss he gave her said much more than that. 'You can have any kind of wedding you want.'

★ ★ ★

They stayed up late, talking about the ceremony and celebration, and even the possibility of a brief honeymoon.

'It should be a civil ceremony,' Gail said.

He nodded. 'Erle can be my best man, Lucy your maid of honor, and your mother can give you away.'

'Then we'll have a reception at the

country club. I'd have it at the house, but I don't want Mother, or Lucy, for that matter, fussing over food and decorations. They should enjoy the occasion right along with us.'

They even began making lists of people to invite to the reception. Hugo, Charles, and Nick, of course.

'If we have Charles and Nick, we have to invite the Seymours,' Gail said.

Charles Walton, their associate in Phoenix, and his cousin, Nick Quintaine, had been raised by their aunt and uncle, the Seymours, who owned the local shopping mall. They had been legal adversaries of Gail's at a much earlier date, but that had all changed. Now they were among their most loyal clients.

'Damon and his wife, and her father,' Gail went on.

She had successfully defended Damon Powell against murder charges, ultimately solving an old crime which had haunted the town for years. He had gone on to attend law school at her urging, had served as her intern, and eventually he had taken over his father-in-law's law firm.

They went down the list, writing in names, scratching a few out, and finally settling on what they thought was a reasonable list. Then they argued back and forth about the possibilities for a honeymoon destination. Gail wanted to go back to San Miguel de Allende in Mexico, where she and Hugo had tracked down their missing witness from the Del Monaco trial, just a few weeks earlier.

'It's gorgeous,' she told Connie. 'You'd love the mission, the streets, the shops, the restaurants . . . I didn't have a chance to take in everything properly. I know we'd have a great time.'

But Connie was holding out for San Francisco and the Bay area. 'There's so much to see and do. The last couple of times we were out there, we ended up spending every moment helping Nick solve his issues, and it was all very traumatic. I'd like to go back just to relax and take in the sights. We could even drive up to the Redwoods and wine country.'

In the end, they agreed to table plans

for a trip for the time being and concentrate on the ceremony itself and the reception.

They went to bed late, tired but happy. Gail slept soundly until just before dawn when her phone buzzed on the nightstand. She nearly knocked it on to the floor, groping for it, but finally got it flipped open.

'Gail Brevard,' she answered automatically.

Her contacts in the police department knew to call her if any of her clients had a mishap.

Or, one of the people from the office might be having a problem. She hoped it wasn't toner needed for the copier.

'Gail,' came a quavering voice, 'Is Connie with you?'

'What's wrong, Lucy?' She sat straight up in bed and turned on the light. 'Is it Erle?'

Connie sat up too, switched his light on, then swung his feet over and found bedroom slippers.

'No,' Lucy said. 'Erle's fine. He's still asleep and I'm trying not to wake him yet. No, Gail, it's your mother . . . '

'Mother . . . ?' Gail could feel her body trembling, as realization sank in. 'Has she . . . ?'

'Your mother passed away peacefully sometime during the night, Gail. I'm so sorry.'

'Have you called anyone yet?'

'No. You're the first one I've called. She seemed a bit . . . off, when we went to bed last night. I went in to check on her just a bit ago. She . . . she was already gone.'

'You're sure . . . ?'

'Yes. I took all her vitals immediately. There's no doubt.'

Lucy was a retired nurse and would have known what to do. 'I didn't call anyone yet because I thought you might want to be here.'

'Yes,' Gail said. 'You did the right thing. We'll be there as quickly as possible. And . . . thank you so much. For everything.' She couldn't say any more.

'I'll be waiting for you,' Lucy said.

Connie was already dressed by the time

she hung up and climbed out of bed. She donned the same outfit she had worn the day before and threw cold water on her face. She didn't care what she looked like. It wasn't important.

Together they shuffled out of the town house and into the parking garage. They didn't say a word while Connie started the car and pulled out into the dark early-morning street.

Finally Gail uttered her first words to him. 'She didn't even know we were going to be married, Connie. She would have been so happy about that.'

Tears ran down her cheeks. She didn't bother to wipe them away.

They were proof of her loss.

⋆　⋆　⋆

The following days were a blur.

First, there was the moment of truth when Gail stood staring down at her mother's still form laid out on the big double bed in the room her parents had shared for as long as she could remember. Lucy had dressed her and fixed her hair.

She looked peaceful and serene, almost as if she had just laid down for a nap.

But there was something not quite right. She was too still, her face pale and waxen. The gnarled hands crossed on her chest were not busy knitting a scarf or chopping vegetables for Sunday dinner.

Her work was done.

Connie stood behind her, ready to provide support, and Lucy pulled the curtain aside a bit, to let in one lone ray of morning sunlight.

'She looks like she's asleep.' Gail's hoarse voice sounded too loud in the silent room.

'I'm sure she didn't suffer,' Lucy said. 'I think she just went to sleep . . . and didn't wake up.'

Gail bent down to kiss her mother's cool cheek and patted the lifeless hands.

'All right,' she said, turning away. 'Let's make the call.'

Lucy led them out of the room and into the den. 'I'll call her doctor and inform him. He may wish to contact the authorities himself. Let me take care of everything. There's coffee on in the kitchen. Why don't you two have a bite to eat? It will get busy soon enough.'

'Thanks, Lucy. I don't think I can eat, but maybe we can fix Erle something. Is he up?'

'He's up but not dressed yet.' Lucy paused. 'I haven't told him, Gail. I wasn't sure how you wanted to handle this.'

Gail started to respond, but Connie put a hand on her shoulder.

'Why don't you let me take care of Erle for a while,' he said. 'I need to do something. You get a cup of coffee and try to relax a little bit . . . before everything gets hectic.'

She tried to flash him a grateful smile but failed. Instead, she just nodded and headed into the living room and collapsed into her mother's favorite easy chair near the window.

I wasn't ready for this, she thought. *But is anyone ever ready?*

How did you prepare for the end of a lifetime?

★ ★ ★

It did not take fifteen minutes before people began arriving and filling up the living area of the house.

First, her mother's physician arrived and hurried quickly into the bedroom to confirm the death. He was followed in turn by various other official vehicles.

The mortuary was contacted. Others were called, including a few of their closest friends, her mother's pastor, the woman who did occasional cleaning for the ladies, the neighbors on either side. Suddenly, the place seemed like a madhouse. All Gail wanted to do was run away and hide somewhere . . . for a very long time. But, of course, she couldn't.

Connie emerged with a very sober Erle, his hair slicked back and dressed in pants and shirt instead of the casual clothes he wore daily for play. Connie had spoken to him at length about the seriousness of the occasion, and he was subdued and trying very hard to look the part of the grown man he resembled instead of the child he had remained.

The cleaning woman arrived with her daughter, and immediately pulled out the biggest coffee urn and got it going. Sandwiches were made and piled on trays on the big granite counter in the kitchen. Quietly the two women went about, straightening the furniture, plumping up pillows, and pulling in extra chairs.

The neighbors showed up and spoke quietly to Connie, offering any kind of assistance needed. The pastor entered.

'Whenever you're ready, we can discuss what your needs will be regarding services,' he said to Gail. 'And please let me know how I can help.'

'Here's Hugo,' Connie said when the minister had moved on to speak with Lucy. 'And look who's with him.'

'Mr. Goldthwaite,' Gail said, holding out her hand. 'Thank you for coming. I really appreciate . . . '

Hugo Goldthwaite, Sr., father of Hugo, Jr., and founder of the Goldthwaite Detective Agency many years earlier, looked down at her.

'Poppa,' the elderly gentleman said, patting her hand. 'Everybody calls me Poppa, and you should, too. I am so sorry, Miss Gail. Your mother was a wonderful lady and a pillar of the community, as they used to say. She will be missed.'

Gail held back the sobs and nodded, holding his hand tightly. She glanced up at the old man and smiled through her tears. 'Thanks,' she whispered to him.

Finally, the authorities completed their deliberations. Everyone stood aside as the gurney was wheeled out bearing the still, cold corpse of Alberta Norris.

It was her final pilgrimage. They all said a silent farewell and wished her safe passage to her new destination.

⋆   ⋆   ⋆

A few days later, they held the funeral. Once again, the community turned out to assist the family and honor a valued member of Cathcart's society.

Gail felt as if she were in someone else's body, greeting old friends and associates, hearing the accolades and words of support and grief, checking occasionally to see that Lucy and Erle were all right.

Connie was a godsend, hovering over her, making sure everything was in order, and seeing to scheduling and event details that were quite simply beyond her at this point.

Somehow they got everyone and everything organized. The funeral was appropriate and tasteful; the burial ceremony, limited to family and a few friends, was gotten through; and the rest of the day was spent receiving well-wishers at the house. The cleaning crew, supervised by Damon Powell's wife, Marilyn, saw to everything. Gail sat with Lucy and Erle on the sofa in front of the living room window and allowed it all to swirl around them.

That evening, after they had retired to the guest room, Connie and Gail took stock.

'We'll need to advance our plans to move out here,' he said. 'We can't leave Lucy on her own, and I think we should also give her the option of returning to her old town and friends, if she'd like.'

'You're right. So long as Mother was alive, she had someone here to back her up and provide adult conversation. I think they genuinely enjoyed each other's company. I know Lucy always said they were more like sisters than cousins. But that dynamic has changed now. We can't leave her here to deal with Erle by herself. That wouldn't be fair.'

Connie placed a supporting arm around her shoulders. 'And I think we need to go ahead with the wedding. Not as we were planning, of course. But I think it's even more important we make that change now.'

'I agree,' she said. 'I think we need to have a very simple ceremony here at the house with just Lucy and Erle. If we did it over the next couple of days, we could ask Charles and Nick while they're still here . . . and Hugo, of course. We'll have just the old gang and no one else. We could do a reception later . . . maybe over the holidays. But not right now.'

So, a few days later, Gail Brevard and Conrad Osterwitz were married by a justice of the peace in the living room of the Norris family home with only five people in attendance. There was no celebration, no reception and no honey-moon.

And that had been the end of August.

4

A taxi pulled up in front of a large two-story house of uncertain vintage on a tree-lined street in the residential area of Newton, a large county seat several hours northwest of Cathcart.

A woman of undetermined age got out, paid the driver and removed a hefty backpack from the car. She refused the cabbie's offer to help her with it.

'I've carried it this far,' she said. 'A few more steps won't hurt me.'

She made her way up the cement walkway from the curb to a wide front veranda. Several old-fashioned wicker rockers were scattered across the painted boards. Lattices at either side of the porch would be covered with sweet-smelling vines in the summer to protect sitters from the sun and nosy neighbors.

Now, in the early stages of winter, the lattices were bare and no vestiges of greenery remained.

She picked one of several keys hanging from the lanyard around her neck, fitted it into the lock and swung the door open. She entered into the dim vestibule and squinted to get her bearings.

A figure emerged from the shadows to greet her. 'Hello, Miss Moreland. So nice to have you back. Do you think you'll be able to stay a little longer this time?'

'I hope so, Mrs. Canty. We'll see.'

'The others are in the parlor, if you want to go in and let them know you're here.'

'Is my room ready?' she said. 'I've been traveling all day. I think I'd like to go up and lie down a bit. Is supper still at 6:00?'

Mrs. Canty had been raised on a farm west of the city and still clung to the country tradition of a hearty dinner at noon and a lighter meal in the evening.

'Yes, ma'am. Everything's just as you left it. Supper's still at 6:00. I'll go ahead and set a place for you.'

'Thank you.'

She hefted her pack again and climbed the stairs to the second floor, stopping a time or two to rest against the dark mahogany bannister. Several bedrooms on either side of the hallway were connected with shared bathrooms, but she was fortunate enough to have one of the larger rooms with an *en suite*. Choosing a second key, she unlocked the door to the last room on the right, entered and looked around.

Everything was, as Mrs. Canty had promised, just as she had left it during her last visit back in July. A comfortable four-poster bed took center stage, surrounded by sturdy old furnishings, including a massive chest of drawers, two matching night stands, a dressing table vanity with triple mirrors and, in front of the window overlooking the side yard, a small writing desk. A comfy easy chair and ottoman upholstered in a large floral pattern sat nearby.

Breathing a sigh of relief, she slid the backpack off her aching shoulders and scooted it out of the way into a corner. She went into the adjoining bathroom, washed her face and brushed her teeth. Back in the bedroom, she pulled the covers back from the bed, slid off her shoes and crawled in.

She fell asleep almost immediately and rested comfortably, without dreaming, for several hours.

At last she awakened, plumped up the pillows and pulled up into a sitting position to review her situation. So far, so good.

She was thankful she had had the foresight and good fortune to have found this place. She had paid for a year's rent in advance, saying she traveled frequently for her job, but wanted the convenience of a place to stay in the area. In July, she had used the excuse to him that she had been asked to attend an out-of-state conference for the university.

He had not doubted her or checked her story, so far as she could tell, and she had stayed here the better part of two weeks, getting acquainted with the other tenants, exploring the bustling city, and making plans for this very day.

Now that she was committed to this course of action, she would be using her secret identity so long as she was here, and wearing the auburn wig . . . at least until she could decide whether or not to dye her own greyish locks.

She rose, changed into one of the fresh outfits she'd left stored in the closet, and made her way downstairs to greet the others.

Smile. She told herself. *It's time for your close-up.*

★   ★   ★

She entered the dining room and took her usual seat at the foot of the sturdy oak table.

Mrs. Canty always sat at the head, next to the swinging doors into the kitchen. Dora Dunn, who worked in the Newton City Library and Jack Williams, who was retired from the railroad, sat to Mrs. Canty's right. Joe Hill, a traveling salesman and Bill Wallace, a teller at the National Bank, sat on her left.

This arrangement never varied, nor had anyone ever asked to change it — nor, as far as she could tell, had anyone ever complained about it. She marveled at how compliant people were in such a situation, reverting completely to habit without question.

'Here she is,' Mrs. Canty said. 'Our Miss Moreland has returned to us.'

There was a general murmur of greeting and smiles flashed across the table at the new arrival.

'I hope you're going to be able to stay a lot longer this time,' said Dora. 'We've *really* missed you.'

'Thank you,' she said. 'But please, call me Ruth. I hate the formality.'

'We missed you, *Ruth*,' said Joe, grinning widely. 'No fun around here without you.'

She smiled back, wondering, as she had so often, why they liked her so much. She guessed it must be the bit of mystery about her background and activities she had spun to keep them off track about her real persona.

'So,' Joe said, 'as Dora said, do you think you're going to be able to stay longer this time?'

She started to answer him then shook her head, as if to clear the cobwebs. Might as well get right into it.

'You know, I've been giving that a lot of thought recently, Joe. I'm really burned out with all the travel. I'm beginning to think I should put down a few roots . . . make an effort to stay in one place for a while. And I can't think of any better spot than this.' She smiled at the faces around the table.

'Would you stay here, do you think?' Dora asked anxiously. 'Or would you try and find a larger apartment?'

'Oh, no.' She tossed her head. 'Give up Mrs. Canty's cooking? Oh my, no. I'd hate to be on my own like that. I'm perfectly happy with the situation here.' Adding yet another lie to the pile already at her feet.

'That's great news,' Jack said, smiling shyly. 'I . . . I've really missed you, too.'

Not for the first time, she wondered if the older man had a bit of a crush on her. She would have to be careful about that.

'The only problem . . . ' They actually all moved forward in their chairs at the hint of difficulty. 'The only problem for me is my income.'

45

There was a communal sigh. They all understood that difficulty only too well.

Mrs. Canty spoke first. 'Well, my dear, as you know, you're paid up for . . . a bit . . . ' She carefully did not reveal how far her roomer was paid up. 'I'm sure we can come to some kind of arrangement for the time being, to help out.'

'Oh, I wouldn't expect any special treatment,' she interposed. 'No, I was thinking more along the lines of finding some sort of job here; something that didn't require travel.'

'Afraid I can't help you out there,' said Joe, the traveling salesman.

Everyone laughed at his little joke.

'I could put your name forward at the bank.' Bill cleared his throat importantly. 'I do have a bit of pull. Of course, they're looking for people with some sort of experience in the financial field, even for starting positions.'

'I doubt I'd qualify for a bank position,' she replied.

The last thing in the world she wanted was to open herself up to any security clearance questions, and she was positive working in a financial institution would require that.

'But,' she went on, glancing shyly at Dora, 'I *was* wondering about the library. What do you think, Dora? Do they ever hire help, temporary perhaps? I'm sure I could do simple filing and office work.'

Dora glowed with self-importance. 'Oh yes, of course! The library is always looking for temporary help, especially in tech services. That's where they get the books ready to go on the shelves . . . and shelving of books . . . filing cards. There's a ton of jobs like that in the library!'

'Why, that sounds perfect. Do you think I could go in with you one morning? You could introduce me and I could look around, see if I think I might be able to handle the work.'

Dora looked as if she was about to burst.

'That would be wonderful, Ruth. We could go to work together; eat our lunch together. We'd have so much fun.'

Poor Dumb Dora, Ruth thought. *She hasn't a clue. But really, I must quit thinking of her like that or I'll slip up one day and actually call her Dumb Dora.*

She knew that Dora took a sack lunch, prepared by Mrs. Canty, every single day. She probably sat out in the quad on nice days and in the employee room on bad, munching away at her peanut-butter-and jelly or bologna sandwich, apple and chips . . . all alone.

Now she would have company; her own 'best' friend at last.

Ruth was beginning to wonder if she had simply traded one prison for another.

'All right,' she said, smiling at poor old Dumb Dora. 'Let's go in together tomorrow morning then . . . the sooner I do this, the better.'

5

Several days earlier, the man known as Jim Peabody bopped along Main Street, swerving from left to right to avoid puddles of melted snow and slush.

The air was brisk and today the sun was blazing down from a bright blue sky, although yet another severe storm had been promised for later in the week. He felt sweaty and messy through his heavy top coat, and the shiny attaché case bounced awkwardly against his leg.

He wished he didn't have to make this call, but it was important — and it could make a huge difference for the future.

He turned north on Court Street and walked half a block further before stopping in front of the elegant white marble façade of the *Sun* building.

The Sun newspaper was nearly as old as the town itself and had had its good years and bad, as well. Today, Cathcart was the seat of the largest county in the state, and home to many influential public offices. And the town's only newspaper was thriving in the current political climate.

Therein lay Jim Peabody's hopes for the future.

He pushed through revolving glass doors, which were twice as tall as he was, and into the busy, warm vestibule beyond. He made his way to the next available clerk and asked directions to the managing editor's office.

'Mr. Weems?' she asked, adding when he nodded, 'Do you have an appointment?'

'Yes. My name's Peabody.'

'Thank you, Mr. Peabody. Mr. Weems' office is at the end of the corridor to your left,' she said, pointing.

He didn't bother to thank her, but turned into the corridor and marched to the end, glancing at the names on the doors as he passed.

Reaching the office at the very end, he turned the knob and pushed his way through. A middle-aged woman was looking through files at the receptionist's desk.

'Yes?' she said, looking up over her glasses. 'May I help you?'

'I have an appointment with Mr. Weems,' he said.

'May I tell him who's calling?'

'Jim . . . James Peabody.'

'Thank you. Please wait here while I see if he's at his desk.' He knew that was code for 'I'll ask if he really wants to see you.'

She went through to the inner office and came back out a moment later. 'He'll see you, Mr. Peabody. Go right in.'

He stepped into what appeared to be an actual working office. Papers and files were scattered about a round conference table in one corner. Chairs were set about, as if a hasty meeting had been called, then broken up just as hastily.

A large man in shirt sleeves sat behind a messy desk, peering intently at the computer screen to one side. He looked up as Peabody entered and gestured to one of the chairs in front of his desk.

'Have a seat, Peabody,' he said. 'What's up?'

'I have some more information for you — about that matter we discussed earlier.'

He reached over and opened the attaché case he had deposited in the chair next to him. Weems eyed the case with doubt. It looked like something a woman would carry.

'All right,' he said. 'Although I must tell you, we're very leery about going ahead with this . . . as a story, I mean. There are too many variables. And it's going to be very difficult to corroborate these claims. I must get an okay from Mr. McAllister before going any further. And I doubt he's going to be that keen on it.'

Robert McAllister was the scion of several generations of owners of *The Sun*. He was not particularly enamored of the job he had inherited, but he loved the money and power it brought. And he would not be at all interested in upsetting the delicate balance between his newspaper and the political bosses of the town of Cathcart — and that most certainly included the current district attorney,

Turner Redland.

'Oh, I understand that,' Peabody said. He paused before continuing, 'But there's a time element here.'

'What do you mean?'

'Well, this information isn't going to just sit there and wait until somebody decides they want to use it, is it? My sources aren't going to be patient little wall-flowers forever. Some of these people have suffered a bit, and at some point they're going to want to get whole again.' He sat back and waited for Weems to digest all this.

'We can't be parties to blackmail, Mr. Peabody,' Sam Weems said firmly. 'And if you're suggesting these so-called 'sources' of yours are only in this for whatever money they might be able to squeeze out of Mr. Redland and his people, then I'm afraid *The Sun* can't — won't — be involved in such a scheme.'

'No, no.' Jim Peabody broke into a sweat. 'I didn't mean to insinuate that we . . . they were going to try and hold the D.A. up over this. It's just that, well, these ladies have suffered some . . . indignities, you know. They really should be compensated for their pain and suffering. A civil suit would be the next step, I believe. I just thought, being privy to all that's going on and all, I just thought the D.A. might want to relieve these young women by getting to the bottom of their complaints. That's all I meant.'

Sam Weems looked at him in doubt. 'Well, I just don't know that we want to get involved in a legal dispute with the D.A.'s office at this point in time. I *can* tell you right now that Mr. McAllister would not be at all happy about that sort of arrangement.'

'Well, why don't you just look over this new information I've brought you, talk it over with McAllister, and get his take on it before you make a final decision?'

Peabody paused. 'Fact is, I couldn't think of anyplace else to go with it, and frankly, I thought the newspaper might well be the best way to handle it as a community service, don't you know?'

The visitor rose, closed the attaché case and shoved the file across the desk to Weems. 'Thanks for seeing me on such short notice,' he said, reaching out to shake the editor's hand.

Weems rose also and shook Peabody's hand briefly before escorting him to the door.

'I'll look over all the materials you've brought again,' the editor said. 'And I'll discuss it with Mr. McAllister as well. I'll let you know our decision within the next several days, but I wouldn't hold out much hope, Peabody. It just doesn't sound like the sort of thing we want to take on right now.'

Jim Peabody nodded and exited the room. He was deeply disappointed. He had thought this would be a sure thing. Obviously he had miscalculated.

Not the first time, he admitted to himself.

Not by a long shot.

6

The morning following the D.A.'s visit, Gail spoke into the intercom connecting her desk with that of her assistant.

'Margaret,'

'Yes, Ms. Brevard?'

'See if you can get Sam Weems at *The Sun* on the phone. I think the number should be on file.'

'I'll try. It's lunch hour right now, so he might be out.'

'Well, give it a try anyway . . . and leave a message asking him to call back if he's out. Thank you.'

She sat back and waited, going over in her mind what Turner Redland had told her about the threats to the D.A.'s office. She had dealt with Sam over other matters, and he had always been forthcoming and cooperative. Maybe he could shed some light on this issue.

Five minutes or so passed before the light on her intercom blinked. 'Yes?'

'Mr. Weems is on the line. I'll transfer you,' came Margaret's crisp voice.

'Thank you, Margaret.' She waited and in a moment there was a distinct click and Sam Weems' gruff voice came over, loud and clear.

'Hello, Gail. Good to hear from you. What can I do for you today?'

'Hi, Sam. Thanks for taking my call, and sorry about bothering you so close to lunch. I hope I'm not interrupting anything.'

'No, it's fine. As a matter of fact, I was just getting ready to go down to Kay's and grab a bite. Would you like to meet me there? Maybe we can combine business and pleasure.'

She glanced at the time showing on her computer screen: 1:10 p.m. 'That sounds great, Sam. I can be over there in about 15 minutes, I think. You go ahead and order and I'll catch up with you.'

Kay's was a popular store-front diner located near the corner of Main and Court streets. They served breakfast and lunch only and catered to the many county and business employees in the area.

At 1:00 the lunch crowd would be cleared out and it would be a perfect place to talk. Besides, she hadn't eaten anything since early that morning, so lunch sounded good.

'Do you want me to send a car for you,' Sam asked. 'It's still pretty slushy out there on the street.'

'No, I'll be fine. The exercise will do me good.'

'Fine; see you there.'

She pulled on her boots, scarf and coat and headed out, leaving instructions with Margaret about where she was going in case Connie or one of the associates needed her.

Crunching along Main Street a few minutes later, she reviewed in her mind again what Turner had said. It was very unlike him to be so concerned about office matters, and she wondered if there was anything else going on that he had neglected to mention to her.

She paused at the corner and waited until the light changed and traffic cleared, then crossed over to Court Street. Here were mostly imposing office buildings interposed with small store-front businesses, like a haberdashery on one side of the street and an exclusive jeweler's on the other. A few steps further down, a neon sign announced that Kay's was 'Open' and she pulled the door and stepped inside.

'Hello, Ms. Brevard,' said a smiling hostess. 'So nice to see you again. Are you meeting anyone?'

'Thanks, Rita. I'm meeting Sam Weems. He may be here already.'

'Yes, he's at his usual booth. You go right on back and I'll bring you a cup of coffee to start.'

'That's fine, and just go ahead and order one of your lunch specials for me. You know what I like.'

'Will do.'

Rita headed toward the kitchen as Gail made her way to the back of the room and joined Sam at his booth.

'Hi, Sam. I made it safely through the slush.' She smiled and shook the hand offered to her.

'Good to see you, Gail. It's been way too long. I really ought to make more of an effort to keep up with everyone. It's a whole different ball game, this editing business, from when I used to get out and about, covering the news.'

'I know what you mean. It's like that for me, too.'

He looked around. 'We need to order for you. Not sure where the waitress is . . .'

'It's all right. I saw her on the way in and went ahead and ordered. She'll bring my coffee.' She smiled as Rita appeared at her side. 'And here she is, right on cue. Thanks, Rita.'

'I brought your special cream, too.' The waitress beamed back. 'Your order will be right up. I told them to put a rush on it.' She turned and hurried on to her other customers.

'Now,' Sam said, as Gail stirred her coffee, 'what can I do for you?'

'I had a visitor in the office yesterday,' she began. 'An unexpected visitor. It was Turner Redland.'

Sam heaved a sigh. 'Ah, yes. I

suspected it might be about that.'

'Sam, he's hired us to investigate allegations that there was something going on in the D.A.'s office that was unacceptable. He indicated that you might have some information about it. I'm just trying to decide if this is just some smoke screen . . . or if there is really something going on that he needs to address.'

'Well, I can tell you what I know, but that isn't a lot,' the editor said. 'A local character named Jim Peabody has come to see me. In fact, he's been in several times. He's obviously just trying to make a buck off this scheme, so I don't know whether to give any credence to his claims, or not.'

'Yes. I think I've heard of him in the police rosters,' Gail said. 'I'm pretty sure he did some time for petty theft at one point. Other than that, he seems to be harmless. But if he's threatening the D.A., that changes things considerably. What's he been saying, if you're free to talk about it?'

'Oh, I think I'm free to talk about it, at

least with you, especially if Redland has hired you. I haven't even gone to McAllister with it, although it may be time for me to do that. I made an 'editorial' decision (he grinned at his little joke) not to pursue this story. At least I won't pursue it yet. Not unless these people go public with their allegations, or try to sue the D.A. or something.'

'These people — so there are several individuals making claims, then. Can you tell me more?'

'You know, for some reason I had a hunch this might be what you wanted to discuss today. I had this stuck in my briefcase, and I brought it along, just in case.' He pulled out a file folder and handed it to her.

'And you're comfortable with me looking at this?'

He smiled. 'If I'm not comfortable with you looking at something, Ms. Brevard,' he said, 'then I'm either a fool or a coward. And I hope you know I'm neither.'

She smiled back. 'And that, Mr. Weems, is a compliment I shall treasure.'

Just then, Rita brought her lunch and she started to hand the file back so she could eat.

'No,' Sam said, 'you keep the file. I'm uncomfortable with it, but I think it needs to be followed up. I think it'd be much better in your hands, especially if Turner has asked for your assistance. Make of it what you will. The only thing I'll want in return will be first dibs on any story coming out of it. Other than that, I think the paper will relinquish this material into your capable custody.'

'Thanks, Sam, for the vote of confidence. You have my word that any story or publicity to come from this, you'll have first call.

'And now, let's eat. I'm starved!'

★ ★ ★

When she had said goodbye to Sam Weems and slushed her way back across Main Street to the office, Gail put in a call to Hugo Goldthwaite.

'Do you have time for a brief

conference? I have a matter we'll need to research.'

'I'm between appointments, Gail,' Hugo said. 'I'll be right down.'

The Goldthwaite Detective Agency, which shared part of the Osterwitz and Brevard office complex, was on permanent retainer with the law firm. More importantly, Hugo, Connie and Gail were close friends and trusted colleagues who had worked on many cases together, most often with successful outcomes. Gail's experience with Hugo, in fact, went back to the earliest days of her career, and he had been a major factor in her first successful stint as a defense attorney.

Connie, as usual, was in court, but she felt it was important to get a handle on the facts in this case as quickly as possible. Turner, in her opinion, had let this go too far. He should have begun investigating these allegations the moment they popped up. She only hoped the delay wouldn't prove fatal to the outcome. The last thing they needed in this town was a tainted district attorney, even one she opposed frequently.

Soon Hugo tapped on the door and stepped in. 'Coffee?' she said, pointing to the bar in the corner.

'No, thanks,' Hugo said. 'I just had a late lunch. Shall we sit at your desk, or is the conference table called for?'

She gestured to the chair across from her desk. 'We can start here. If it looks like we'll need more space for notes, we can move.'

He took his place and looked with curiosity at the folder she handed to him. In it were the notes she had taken when she first spoke with Turner, a copy of the receipt for her services, and the somewhat more voluminous documents she had just received from Sam Weems. They sat in silence a few minutes while Hugo reviewed the file. Finally, he closed the folder and looked up.

'I've heard of this guy, Jim Peabody,' he said. 'He's got a bad reputation. Nothing violent, at least as far as anyone knows. But he's always been on the wrong side of the law; things like petty theft, shady gambling deals, and minor swindling schemes. If it wasn't for the target here, I'd say it probably doesn't amount to a hill of beans. Given that he's gone after a government official this time, I'd say this looks a little more serious. What's Turner's position?'

'He says he knows nothing about any of it,' Gail said. 'The employees involved are all low-level temp workers. Now I'm wondering if they were all supplied by the same company.' She made a note to herself to follow up on that thought. 'Also,' she continued, 'Turner claims he's never had any complaints from any of his regular long-term employees. I tend to believe him, Hugo. As much as I detest the man personally, this doesn't sound like anything he'd allow to go on in his office. I could be wrong about that, though.'

'Tell you what. Let me make copies of all this.' Hugo tapped the file on the desk in front of him. 'And I'll try and figure out what's going on with Mr. Peabody and his friends.'

'I don't have to warn you, of course,'

Gail said, 'that tins must be kept under wraps. This is politically sensitive stuff, and we've got to be careful not to tip any of these people off.'

He smiled at her. 'You know me, Boss. Mum's the word. I'll be as silent about this as the proverbial church mouse.'

She laughed. 'Right. Now let's get these things copied and get you on your way so you don't miss your next appointment.'

Copies in hand, Hugo left to return to his office, and Gail sat looking thoughtfully into space. What *was* going on in the D.A.'s office? she wondered. And where would Hugo's investigations lead? If Turner Redland was involved in mistreating his employees, or even allowing it to go on with his tacit approval, what did that say about her ability to read the people in her orbit? More importantly, what did it say about the whole system? Were they up against something much more nefarious with implications more far-reaching than they had suspected?

She sighed and returned to her computer. But it was a long time before she could settle down and get back to work on the case at hand.

That was the problem with new cases. They were almost always more enticing than the current ones.

7

The very next morning after their discussion at Mrs. Canty's dinner table, Ruth Moreland and Dora Dunne, like schoolgirls, headed out early to catch the bus to the Newton City Library. Each was dressed conservatively and nearly identically, in neat dark pantsuits and sturdy flat shoes, and each lady carried, along with a serviceable shoulderbag, a brightly colored lunch kit packed lovingly by Mrs. Canty.

Dora was vociferous, explaining the intricacies of the bus transfer they would need to make before reaching downtown. Ruth kept quiet about the intra-state bus pass she still had stashed away in her backpack in the nether regions of her closet. She didn't think Mrs. Canty would stoop to snooping into her things, but she couldn't be altogether sure of that. She had hidden her documents away as stealthily as she could, but there was little

69

option, really, in how safe they truly were from curious eyes.

Ruth tuned out Dora's non-stop comments as much as possible, nodding pleasantly and saying 'Yes' whenever there was a pause, which wasn't often. Finally, after the mid-town transfer, their bus rolled up to its final destination.

'Downtown,' called the driver. 'All out.'

They tumbled down the bus steps in the company of other early-morning employees off to face another day on the job.

'This way,' commanded Dora, pointing to a side street angling away from the busy downtown traffic. 'This is quicker than going in the front.'

'Will they let me in through the employees' entrance?' Ruth asked. 'Won't I need I.D. of some kind?'

'Nonsense! You're with me. They know me and I'll vouch for you. They'll let you in all right.'

She strode self-importantly ahead of the wavering Ruth, who did not want to start her interview on a bad note. But Dora was correct. The security personnel knew her and didn't seem at all concerned that she was dragging in someone new through the employee door.

'Fine, go ahead,' said the woman checking them through. 'Take the lady to H.R. if she's got an appointment.'

Ruth *didn't* have an appointment, but Dora was adamant that there would be no problem in seeing someone. The library was always looking for competent help, and she'd never known them to turn anyone away just because they didn't have an appointment.

Dora muscled her way in to the human resources office, spoke quickly to the young intern on duty, and marched on through to the inner sanctum, motioning Ruth to follow.

'Good morning,' an attractive grey-haired woman greeted them from a desk fronted by two upholstered side chairs. 'Hello, Dora. Who's this?'

'Good morning, Mrs. Long. This is Ruth Moreland. She's rooming with me and is looking for a job. I suggested she try here before putting her application in elsewhere. I know you're always looking for good employees, and I can recommend her highly.'

Ruth stepped forward, looked directly into the older woman's eyes and offered her hand. Frances Long touched her fingers briefly and motioned her to one of the chairs. She glanced over at Dora.

'All right, Dora, you can go on in to work now. Thank you for seeing Ms. Moreland in and introducing her.'

Dora, disappointed she was not to be part of the negotiations, nodded and whispered to Ruth, 'See you later for lunch,' as she made her way out the door.

'Now then, Ms. Moreland . . . '

'Ruth, please.' She smiled.

The other woman relaxed and leaned back in her chair. 'Why don't you just tell me a bit about yourself and why you think you'd like working in our library.'

Ruth relaxed too, and proceeded to spin her well-prepared tale of her educational background and employment.

'Do you have references from your most recent position?' Mrs. Long asked.

'Unfortunately, I don't. I've only

recently decided to leave the line of work I've been in because I no longer wish to travel all the time. And since I wasn't allowed to disclose my employer because it was a 'secret shopper' type of position, I thought it wiser I not discuss my current plans with them. It just seemed . . . better, under the circumstances.'

'I see. Ordinarily, we require references of some sort.'

'Well, I do have letters of recommendation from both my landlady, Mrs. Canty, who has been in her line of work for many years, and also from Mr. William Wallace, who is currently employed in a position of trust at the National Bank here in town.'

She produced the letters, composed and pounded out on Joe's old typewriter the prior evening. Frances Long studied the two documents thoughtfully.

'These are quite glowing testimonials,' she said, looking up at last. 'These people, as well as Dora, seem to think very highly of you.'

Ruth ducked her head, as if embarrassed.

'Well, I *like* people. I suppose they see

that and it makes them feel comfortable with me.' That was probably the most honest statement she had made up to now.

'All right, Ms. Moreland — Ruth, if I may. I'm willing to give you a try. How soon could you start?'

'As soon as possible. Today even, if I can. I don't like being idle.'

Frances Long laughed. 'You won't have any problem finding things to do here,' she said. 'There's always some job or other. Jo-Ella, the intern in the outer office, will give you some paperwork to fill out then take you down and introduce you to the person in charge of the area where you'll start.'

She hesitated. 'You didn't mention what kind of salary you're expecting.'

'Whatever you normally pay someone like me will be fine,' she said.

'Good. We'll start you at our regular rate' She named a modest amount. 'I think we can give you 30 hours a week to begin with. You'll be on probation your first month, of course, and, I'm sorry to say, we pay in arrears. You won't receive a full check until you've worked a full month. Will that be a problem for you?'

'No. I'll be all right for a month.'

Actually, this was much better than she had anticipated. She would be able to stay here as long as necessary until she figured out her next move.

She stood, smiled again, and shook Frances Long's hand. 'Thank you,' she said. 'You have no idea how much this means to me.'

★ ★ ★

The routine at the library was easy for her, as it should have been. It was mostly sorting and filing, things she could do almost by rote.

For some strange reason, the Newton City Library was stuck in the last century, organization-wise. They still used old-fashioned card catalogs because, as the lady in charge of tech services explained, 'Our patrons prefer using the cards over the computer resources. We have computer access, of course, but nobody wants to look things up that way. We'll have to wait another few more years, I guess, before we can begin to make some of the changes that will bring us into the current way of doing things.'

She heaved a sigh and waved at the stacks of cards.

'The most difficult part is finding people who can alphabetize properly. You'd be surprised how many of the students and interns don't know their ABCs.'

She smiled at the lady. 'Well, I know them, and I don't have a problem with working with the cards. Just show me what needs to be done and I'll have a crack at it.'

'Great. Here, you grab a stack of these and start putting them in order. I'll check your first batch out. If it all looks okay, you can go ahead and do as many as possible before taking your lunch. If you can work until 4:00 p.m., that will be great. We can find plenty for you to do.'

Ruth got started and quickly ran through the first stack and took them over to be checked.

'These are perfect. No mistakes that I

see. You're free to go ahead and work as much as you like on these. I'll gradually give you other things to do as well, just so you don't get bored.' She gave a little laugh.

'Oh, I won't get bored. I like to keep busy,' Ruth said, quickly grabbing another pile.

She would do anything to take her mind off the cold reality of her situation . . . anything at all to keep the shadows of doubt from her door.

★   ★   ★

The work was mindless, which suited her. An hour or two into the job, the other students and interns were coming to her with questions about procedure. She began keeping a list of their questions and her answers, especially if she had done any research to find the correct response.

By late morning she had a full page of questions and answers. Rose Travens, the woman supervising the interns, looked over her shoulder and nodded.

'Ruth,' she said, 'I'd like you to move over to that spare computer and run your list off for me. Go ahead and make a dozen or so copies of it. I think we can use that in our orientation and training program.'

'Yes, ma'am,' she said. She picked up her materials and took a seat at the computer. Soon it was up and running. Rose showed her a few commands linked to the library's use and she quickly typed in the question list, put a header on it, 'Frequently Asked Questions,' and ran off a dozen copies. She turned off the computer, placed the copies in a file folder, and delivered them to the supervisor's desk.

'Is that all, Ms. Travens?' she said.

Rose looked over her handiwork and smiled. 'Good job, Ruth. Thank you very much. I think these will help.'

Ruth started to turn away but Rose stopped her. 'I'd like you to take these on up to the reference desk on the first floor,' the supervisor said. 'Explain them to the person on duty there and ask them to call me. I suspect you're going to be of more use to us in public services. Is that all right with you?'

'Yes, ma'am,' she said. 'I'd be very happy to help out wherever you think best.'

Dora was dumbfounded when Ruth gave her the news at lunchtime.

'Well,' she said, 'that was certainly quick. I don't think I've ever heard of anyone coming in as an intern being moved upstairs so fast. You must have done a bang-up job this morning.'

Dora seemed happy for her, but Ruth could detect a little note of jealousy. She'd have to be careful not to be too successful in the library. She couldn't risk putting Dora's nose out of joint. She needed all the friends she could get these days.

'Oh, I don't know, Dora,' she said, taking another bite of her peanut butter and jelly sandwich. 'I suspect it was just a fluke. They probably needed some extra help upstairs, and I just happened to be in the right place at the right time.'

The fact that in real life she was a university professor with a PhD in

English Lit might have helped also. She missed teaching and her students, more than she ever thought she would. But maybe this bit of a job would help make up for the sudden lack of motivation in her life. After all, there was more than one path to making a contribution to education.

She would make lemonade out of lemons if need be.

★   ★   ★

On the next day, several other changes took place.

Most obvious was the fact that she was told to come in to work through the main door instead of the downstairs employee entrance. This was a little disconcerting to Dora, who considered it somewhat of an affront that she, too, couldn't come in at the front with Ruth.

'I think they just see it as the quickest, most convenient route for me,' Ruth said. 'I don't think it means anything at all.'

But the next innovation was much more problematical. The time for her lunch break was changed to a half hour later, which meant she could no longer share that time with Dora in the employee lunch room.

Several of the staff on the first floor approached and asked if she would like to join them at the diner across the street. She quickly said yes, before wondering if that would be a mistake.

By the time they got back to the boarding house that evening, Dora was scarcely speaking to her.

'Whatever is wrong with that girl?' said Mrs. Canty. 'Dora's gone straight to her room. That's not like her. Is she sick, do you think?'

Ruth shrugged. 'The library has asked me to change my lunch time so Dora and I won't be able to eat together any longer. Also, I won't be taking a lunch tomorrow, as I've been asked to join the others for lunch outside the library.'

Mrs. Canty shook her head. 'Poor Dora. She's been dying for a friend at work. I'm sure she thought you and she would get along just fine. Looks like that's not going to be the case.'

Ruth thought about the situation. In fact, she thought about it a lot that evening. She wondered now if Dora would even sit with her on the bus.

Dora did not come down to supper, and later Mrs. Canty took a tray up to her room.

'Poor mite,' she said when she came back down. 'She's just sitting there moping. I don't know what we're going to do with her.'

The more Ruth thought about it, the more worried she became. She could not afford to alienate anyone here in the boarding house, even Dumb Dora. And if it meant eating a little crow to heal the breach, then that was what she must do.

Later that evening before going to bed, she tapped on Dora's door after discerning a light under the crack.

'Yes?' came a wavering voice.

'Dora, it's me, Ruth. May I come in and speak with you for a minute?'

There was a brief silence before Dora responded. 'All right, come on in.'

She opened the door and entered Dora's domain. There were clothes strewn everywhere, on the dressing table, the chair . . . even the floor. Dora was sitting up in bed looking messy and disheveled, an open novel lay at her side, and the remains of dinner still sat on a tray on her night stand.

'What do *you* want?' Dora said.

Ruth pulled the straight chair out from the desk, turned it toward the bed, and sat down. 'I wanted to apologize to you for any misunderstanding today,' she said.

Dora stared at her. 'It wasn't my idea to change my lunch time. But because I'm so new, I didn't think it was wise to argue with them about it. I think now I should have said something, and I intend to do so tomorrow. I'm going to ask if I can have my old lunch time back . . . or if not, if your time can be changed to mine. I don't know what they'll say. They may even let me go over it. But I don't want anything to come in the way of our friendship.'

She paused and took a deep breath. She hadn't really thought all that through before she said it, but it seemed evident to her that the most urgent thing right now was to retain the goodwill of the people in the boarding house.

If she lost the job, so be it. She could probably find another, but if not, she would probably be gone from here anyway at some point in time. If it was sooner rather than later, what possible difference could it make?

Dora sniffed. She was actually shedding tears!

'Oh, Ruth,' she said, 'you're truly a wonderful friend. I don't know why I doubted you. I'll go with you to make the request. I don't think they'll want to lose both of us.'

Probably not, Ruth thought. The library administration would probably acquiesce in their request, just to keep everyone happy. And she would continue having peanut-butter sandwiches in the employees' room with Dumb Dora instead of lunch specials at the diner with stimulating colleagues.

She thought, *What have you done? Whatever have you done?*

8

On the very same day that Ruth Moreland had begun her trek to the Canty Boarding House in Newton, Gail Brevard and Conrad Osterlitz had been seated at one end of the conference table in Gail's office reviewing various client files, their tense faces reflected in the smooth polished-wood surface. Then a brief knock came at the door.

'Come in,' Connie said.

They watched in curiosity as Hugo entered, followed by a middle-aged man clad in an ill-fitting darkish suit of indeterminate vintage. He was sweating profusely, and quickly grabbed the bottle of water offered him and took a couple of hefty gulps before sprawling in one of the upholstered chairs ringing the table.

'Ms. Brevard and Mr. Osterwitz,' Hugo said, by way of introduction, 'this is James Peabody.

'He's agreed . . . ' Hugo paused before

continuing to look meaningfully at Peabody, who was avoiding direct contact with the detective's eyes.

'Mr. Peabody has agreed to speak with us *informally* about his recent overtures to Sam Weems at *The Sun Company* about matters alleged to have taken place in the district attorney's office. That's right, *isn't it*, Jim?'

Peabody leaned forward, unbuttoned his suit jacket and eyed the paperwork on the table. 'Well, yeah . . . er, yes,' he said. 'That's what I've agreed to.' He grabbed the water bottle again, took another swig, and wiped his brow with a wilted handkerchief. 'Nothing *official*, mind you,' he continued. 'I don't want any records of anything I say to be made any part of anything official, understand?' He glared in Gail and Connie's direction.

Gail studied him. He was every bit the con man, a type she had come to know and loathe throughout her career. But she knew how to handle him. They could all be handled, if you just found the right angle.

'Of course, Mr. Peabody,' she said,

smiling sweetly. 'This is definitely not a formal deposition. Nothing you say here will be used against you legally, or in any other way to compromise your position, whatever that may be. We're just trying to get a handle on things . . . figure out what the best approach will be to settle your friends' claims — amicably, if possible.'

He relaxed a bit and leaned back in the chair. 'Well, that's all right then. I just don't want you legal types to take advantage of me, coming here all alone and without representation. Believe you me, I had a real hesitation about doing that.'

His eyes rolled around to where Hugo was standing nearby. Hugo didn't react or smile in any way. Peabody shrugged.

'I guess this won't hurt noth — anything. I'm just trying to do some people I know a favor, that's all. I don't have a dog in the hunt, so it don't — it doesn't matter to me what you all do about this.'

'Fine,' said Connie. 'I'll stipulate that we aren't recording this conversation, and you'll be able to look at whatever notes we might take and verify that they reflect your actual words and position. In fact, we'll *insist* that you sign an affidavit at the end of this meeting stating that you agree that everything discussed here is exactly as you stated. Are we straight on that?'

The attorney smiled at Peabody, but his eyes were deadly serious. Peabody glanced back at Hugo. No help there.

'Yeah — Yes. I agree. Let's get this over with. I've got other things to do today.'

'So do all of us, Mr. Peabody,' said Gail, suddenly business-like.

She shuffled the papers in front of her together and called in Margaret, who took her place seated just behind Gail. Gail began dictating in a monotone the facts of the meeting: date, time of day, who was present; and Margaret quickly wrote it all down.

'Now, Mr. Peabody,' she said, 'let's get started. How did you first become aware of the people who are now making these claims against the district attorney's office? Did they come to you? And why? Why would they believe that you were the one who could assist them with their claims?'

And so it went. For at least an hour, Jim Peabody was questioned. He went through another bottle or two of water, and Margaret filled up several pads. Finally, they stopped for a break and Margaret left to type up her notes. Peabody used the restroom. Gail got up and stretched and headed for the coffee bar. Hugo and Connie huddled together discussing what they had learned.

Finally, Margaret returned with her notes and Peabody sat down again to review them. After a few minutes, he looked up.

'This all looks fine to me,' he said. 'I'm okay with what's here. Where do I sign?'

Hugo produced a pen and pointed to the spot on the page where Peabody would acknowledge that these were indeed his words and that nothing had been materially altered. He signed and dated the document and handed it back.

'All right, then,' he said with a sigh of relief. 'I guess that's all. Now, if you don't have anything else . . . '

He got up and moved toward the door but Hugo stepped in front of him, blocking the way.

'Just stay where we can get hold of you if necessary,' said Hugo. 'And I wouldn't mention anything about this meeting to anyone else, either.'

It was all said in a low-key manner, but Hugo never cracked a smile — and Jim Peabody didn't either. They looked at each other steadily for a few seconds before Peabody cast his eyes downward.

Hugo tucked a folded bill into Peabody's pocket and stepped back out of the way. The older man seemed very uncomfortable with the detective's actions, but didn't make any attempt to return the money to him.

Peabody spoke again. 'Ms. Brevard, Mr. Osterwitz,' he said, 'it's been a real pleasure. Very happy to make your acquaintance. I hope what I had to say today will be of help in your . . . your investigations.'

'Thank you, Mr. Peabody,' Connie said. 'We'll be in touch if we need anything further from you.'

Jim Peabody scurried out of the office,

down the hall and back into obscurity.

It was the last they saw of him.

★   ★   ★

As the door closed on Jim Peabody, another door opened to the adjoining office, and Turner Redland stepped into the room.

'Well,' he said, 'that was interesting.'

'My first recommendation,' Gail said, 'is to get rid of the temp employment agency which has been providing the workers in question. This is clearly a scam. The only other question we should consider right now is if the D.A.'s office is the only target for these people, or if they're doing this to other organizations — and, even more importantly, why? Is this just a money-making scheme, or are there other motives?'

Hugo spoke up. 'I'll get my people on to this right away. And I think one of the law-enforcement agencies should start figuring out how to shut them down altogether. I think Gail's right. You may not have been the only organization tagged by them.'

'Agreed,' said Turner, 'with both suggestions. I'll get my people working on it from the official end of things.'

Connie nodded. 'Any suggestions on which of your agencies might be a good fit for putting a stop to their operations?'

'I've been thinking about it. I'm wondering if this might fit into the parameters of Sheriff Carter. He's been chomping at the bit for a 'project,' especially since he'll be up for re-election next term. What do you all think? This is a new one for me. I feel like I'm boxing my way out of a paper bag.'

'I think you should move very carefully,' Gail said, 'especially with your existing employees. You don't want to give any of them an excuse to file a grievance or lawsuit against you personally.'

Turner sighed. 'How could I have let this happen?' he said. 'I'm angry at myself for being such an idiot. Here I've prided myself for years on running a tight ship and being an exemplary boss.'

'Don't be too hard on yourself,' said Hugo. 'These kinds of scams go on all the time. Most of us are just fortunate if we don't get blindsided and taken in by all the grifters and con men out there. Believe me, I've seen enough of this kind of garbage to last me a lifetime.'

After making sure they all had copies of the notes taken during Peabody's dissertation, Turner shook hands with each of the others and thanked them for their support before turning to make his way out of the office.

'I presume you'll be in touch with how your investigations move forward,' he said. 'And I'll do the same with anything I might discover as well.'

'Yes,' said Connie. 'Be sure to let us know if you hear anything or if anyone begins acting suspiciously. We can't afford to let this get out of hand. There's a lot at stake here.'

'Thanks, Connie,' Turner said, grasping the other man's hand. 'I really appreciate the effort you all are making here.'

'It isn't just for you,' Gail spoke up. 'The integrity of your office is at risk here, too. I know we've been on the opposite side at times, but I've never doubted your integrity. This town can't afford to lose confidence in the office, not just the man. This issue is important for all of us. And I think we have to look at it that way.'

Turner nodded. 'You're right, of course. I won't be district attorney forever. But Cathcart needs and deserves to be represented before the law by an organization it can trust and rely upon. Even a hint of corruption or wrongdoing could be fatal to our whole system of justice. We must put a stop to it before that happens.'

He shook hands with each of them again and left the office. *Looks like it might snow tonight*, he thought, pulling up the collar of his overcoat against the cold.

He moved down the hallway and out into the street, following in the footsteps of his nemesis, Jim Peabody, wondering when and if their paths would cross again.

9

In Newton the next morning, Ruth, as promised, and accompanied by an eager Dora, entered the office of Frances Long, the woman who had hired her.

'Come in, ladies,' the supervisor said. 'I understand there's something you wish to discuss with me.'

'Thank you for seeing us on such short notice,' Ruth said. 'There's a matter that's come up with my scheduling that's a bit of a problem for us.'

'Oh, I'm sorry to hear that.'

The older woman looked at Ruth with concern. She had heard good things about the new hire and hoped they would be able to keep her for a while at least. Everyone always moved on from these starter positions, but the longer they could keep the good ones, the better for the library.

'Yes,' Ruth continued. She had urged Dora to stay quiet and let her do the talking.

'You see, when I started here, Dora and I wanted to spend as much of our time together as possible. She's made me feel so welcome in my new home, and she's the one who suggested I might enjoy working here. I owe her everything, really.'

'I see,' Frances said, with a hint of doubt in her voice. 'How can I help?'

'It's very simple, really. Because of the change in my duties, I've been asked to take my lunch break at a slightly different time. When I started here, one of the things that became such a plus for me was the fact that I could take my lunch with Dora. You see, our landlady fixes our lunches for us every day, and we're accustomed to eating together. Now we can't do that any longer.'

'Oh, I see.' Frances was a bit puzzled. These two women did not seem at all compatible to her. But then what did she know?

Frances Long sat for a moment before making a quick decision. 'Let's see if we can fix that. Ask your supervisor to give me a call when you get back to the desk.

I'm sure it won't make that much difference when you take your lunch break.'

'Oh, thank you so much,' Ruth said, standing and offering her hand.

Dora stepped forward also and mumbled a few words that sounded like 'Thanks a lot.'

'That's all right,' Frances said. 'You'd probably better get back to what you were doing. Have a good day.'

'Yes, ma'am. You, too.'

Ruth grabbed Dora by the elbow and shepherded her out the door before she could say anything further to Frances Long. She waited until they got in the elevator and hit the button for the ground floor.

'Now,' she said, 'i've fixed it. We'll still be able to eat lunch together. Let's talk no more about it.'

Dora looked at Ruth curiously. Something seemed not quite right about her new best friend. She wondered, and not for the first time, if she really knew this woman named Ruth Moreland.

And if she didn't know the new

boarder as well as she thought, what secrets were being hidden from her?

★ ★ ★

But Ruth had other things on her mind, staring out the bus window on the way home from the library that evening.

Earlier that very day, she had been shown the patrons' reading room, and as part of her new tasks had been assigned the job of straightening up the magazines and newspapers every morning at opening.

The library received daily newspapers from all the major cities — Los Angeles, New York, Chicago and others — along with those from large towns within the state.

The Cathcart Sun was one of them.

The newspapers were first draped over racks in several large wooden cabinets placed about the room, resembling nothing so much as the day's laundry hung out to dry. Every morning, the previous day's papers were removed to storage areas and replaced by the new

98

morning's editions. Patrons could thus get their daily news from various sources and cities all over the country throughout the day.

Ruth was happy with the new assignment. She quickly realized that it was going to be a mindless task which would have her on her own into a quiet area and give her a bit of time to think about her day. As she worked with the newspapers, though, she was reminded of the hours she had put in at the university last year, plowing through cards of microfiche dating from around the time of her own birth. Finally, just when she had been about to give up, she found the one she needed — a birth announcement for baby girl Ruth Ann Moreland in a small town in the northern part of the state. Then, tragically, several weeks later, an article noted that baby Ruth and her parents had all perished in an automobile crash. The parents had been Canadian immigrants who had no immediate family members in the area.

She had moved quickly to secure both a certified copy of the birth certificate from the local recorder, and a new Social Security card in the same name. There was no reason to believe, after this length of time, that anyone was still left to question the identity of an adult Ruth Moreland living and working in Newton.

Before daring to make her getaway from Cathcart, she had taken the precaution earlier to schedule an extended family leave from her position at the university, pleading the case of a fictitious elderly and seriously ill relative who resided in another state. The time off would cover her absence up to and through the holidays. In any case, the university was closed the last two weeks of the year as an economic measure, and she would not be expected back to work until mid-January, when orientation and classes stalled up again.

Also, she had counted heavily on the probability that she would not be reported missing so long as her salary was still being paid into the bank account she held jointly with him. In the months since last July, she had skimmed off as much as she possibly could from that mutual account without being too obvious, and during the final weeks before her sudden departure she had closed out her 401k and Money Market accounts as well.

Altogether, she had managed to save up a nice little nest egg over the last few years, even with the larger portion of her salary going into the checking account she shared with him. He had never questioned how much money she earned, so long as he was able to easily access and spend it. And that was a topic she had never raised with him.

But once the university began questioning her unapproved absence at the beginning of the coming year, it would certainly become an issue with the authorities. She had counted on being settled enough here in Newton by then that her new identity wouldn't be questioned.

Now, she thought, what if a story about her disappearance was publicized in the Cathcart newspaper — or in any of the other papers throughout the region? Surely a photograph of her would be included, possibly on the front page. Had

101

she disguised herself well enough that she wouldn't be recognized by all these people with whom she was now interacting on a daily basis?

On the way back to the boarding house that evening, as Dora babbled away aimlessly at her side and she gazed with unseeing eyes through the smudged window into murky twilit streets, the woman now known as Ruth Moreland was having second thoughts about the whole plan.

Suddenly a cold sweat came over her. She felt dizzy and disoriented. Could all of her well-planned schemes be so easily undone? Why hadn't she thought of this simple possibility? She had done a huge thing to escape from an existence that had become too painful to bear. Had she only traded one hell for an even worse fate?

Only time would tell, she thought, as she and Dora disembarked and trudged down the street toward the flickering porch lights guiding them back to Mrs. Canty's boarding house.

'Gee,' said Dora, shivering in the cold,

'it's getting so dark in the evening. That time of the year I guess. Almost time for the hobgoblins to appear!'

10

'Did something seem odd to you about Hugo?' Gail said to Connie at dinner later that evening. 'I thought he was a little obvious when he warned Peabody about leaving town.'

'Yeah, I was going to mention that.' Connie stirred his coffee thoughtfully.

'And what was that bit about the money? We hadn't agreed to pay the guy to talk to us. Did Hugo make a separate agreement with him, just to get him to come in and cooperate?'

'I don't know. Not something I suggested, for sure.'

She sat staring at her plate with unseeing eyes.

'I think maybe we'd better have a talk with him about it. It's very unlike him to go off solo like that. He should have mentioned it to us at least.'

Connie shook his head.

'Also, I thought Turner seemed a bit

reserved when he left. I hope we haven't gotten ourselves into a difficult position here. It isn't every day, after all, that we take on defending the district attorney and his whole organization.'

Gail didn't say anything, but she felt uncomfortable. Connie was right; they probably should have referred this back to Turner. He was capable of doing his own investigation and follow-up if necessary.

They finished dinner and headed out to the Norris house. Not only were they maintaining their regular work schedule, but they were trying to oversee the finishing details on the remodeling of Gail's family home for their own use.

Lucy had immediately responded to their overtures with an emphatic request to stay on as Erle's caretaker. 'I love him. I love the both of you, and I'm as comfortable as I can possibly be here,' she said.

'Yes, I've maintained ties to my old friends and colleagues up north. But I made my decision when I moved down here. I am so thankful for the time I had with Alberta, and I'm committed to caring for Erle as long as I'm able . . . that is, if you both are all right with it, too.'

Gail hugged her. 'Of course, it's all right with us,' she said. 'We just wanted to give you the option to do as you wish. Your home is with us for as long as you want it to be.'

And so with that detail decided, they had moved ahead, the three of them, with plans for updating and improving the existing house into something that would work well for all of them. In the end, their plans did not prove to be that extensive. And they all acknowledged that their needs for change were not that great.

The footprint of the house would remain the same, with small accommodations made inside for the convenience and happiness of everyone, including Erle. But the interim period of painting, hammering and miscellaneous decorating had been demanding on all of them. Gail, for one, would be relieved when they were through with all the upset and could settle in and relax for a change.

They had decided to retain the town house for many reasons. It gave them a place to house out-of-town guests and witnesses, but most importantly, they would still be able to stay in town during extended trials or periods of intensive research. Anyone from the office could now eat lunch, take a nap, or simply relax for a few hours without interruption.

For now, Gail and Connie were still spending most of their weeknights in town. But very soon they would be making the final move to the suburbs.

And that day could not come soon enough for all of them.

★　★　★

Sleep did not come easily to Gail that night.

She kept reviewing, over and over in her mind, those last few moments of the day when Hugo sent Jim Peabody off with a cryptic warning, and Turner Redland followed the older man out with a strange look on his face. What was going on?

One thing Gail was certain of. She and Connie would have to have a conversation with Hugo and get to the bottom of what was going on between him and James Peabody. They could not allow any irregularities to jeopardize the case they were developing with the district attorney.

And what of Turner himself? Why did he seem so circumspect? Was there more to this situation than met the eye?

She turned over, fluffed her pillow, and tried to go back to sleep. But still she had dreams about being chased through an underground garage by men who were strangers with familiar faces. She woke, hungover and headachy, but determined to put an end to the doubts plaguing her.

'Connie,' she said, shaking him out of a sound sleep, 'get up. We've got a lot to do today. Get Hugo on the phone first. He can meet us for an early breakfast. I'm going to get to the bottom of all this nonsense, or know the reason why.'

A short while later, a grumpy Hugo met an equally grumpy Connie and a hyper Gail at their favorite coffee shop near the office.

'What's up, boss?' he said, reaching for the cup of hot black coffee plunked down in front of him. 'Sounded like an emergency when you called and got me out of bed this morning. I sure hope this was worth it.'

Connie stared pointedly at Gail. 'Ask the real boss,' he said. 'She's the one with all the answers.'

Gail didn't respond immediately, but contented herself to peruse the menu while the two men eyed her impatiently. Finally she put it aside and looked Hugo squarely in the eye.

'What in the world was going on between James Peabody and you yesterday?' she said. 'I felt like I was taking part in a scene out of *The Godfather*. You know how much is riding on this investigation. We're not only dealing with the integrity of the district attorney's office and position, but we're also trying to protect the reputation of an old acquaintance. If you know more about this guy Peabody than you're letting on, you need to tell us now. And I mean everything.'

Gail seldom let her anger get the best of her, but she was close to it now. The more she had thought about it, the more frustrated she had become. If she couldn't rely upon one of her oldest friends and colleagues to be honest with her and keep her informed, who could she depend on?

Hugo stared into his cup for a moment. 'I'm sorry, Gail ... and you, too, Connie,' he said. 'That was a bad call on my part. I had my reasons, but you're absolutely right. I should have let you know what was going on.'

'And?' Gail fixed him with stormy eyes. 'And what is that supposed to mean?'

Connie stirred next to her. This whole conversation was making him very uncomfortable. Two of his favorite people in the whole world were at odds, and that was a situation he could not bear.

'Hear him out, Gail,' he said. 'Give him a chance.'

'All right.' She shrugged. 'Go ahead, Hugo. I'm all ears.'

'To begin with,' Hugo said, 'I wasn't sure if he was the same guy at all. I mean, he *looked* like the Jim Peabody I'd seen

110

around town from time to time. But there was something just a little different about him.'

Connie frowned. 'You mean you don't think this guy was actually James Peabody?'

Hugo paused, struggling to find the right words. 'It was his mannerisms that seemed different to me.' He sipped his coffee thoughtfully before continuing. 'Let me explain. The guy I used to see around town, the one I knew as Jim Peabody, was laid back, easygoing, and definitely not a vicious type. He just liked to cut corners a bit. I've never used him as a source, at least not that I remember. But he always seemed to me to be a bit of a loser. Minor gambling, petty theft and larceny, you get the picture.'

'But what changed, Hugo? What was so different about him this time?'

'When I began asking around, trying to track him down to bring him in for our conference, I began getting mixed signals. Half the people I spoke with remembered him the way I did — not too bright or trustworthy, but of no real threat to anyone but himself.'

'And the other half?' Connie asked.

'Others, especially those who had had more recent dealings with the man, were not as kind in their assessments. In fact, some people were very forthright in their opinions. And a few stated they actually despised him.'

'Why?'

Hugo had raised Gail's curiosity now. 'Did any of them know why he'd changed?'

'Not really. All I could ascertain was that he had become deliberately mean in his actions. Eventually, I spoke with one of my former female operatives, and it was a real eye-opener.'

Gail held her breath. 'What do you mean?'

'She'd left my employ about two years ago to go with a larger outfit up north. At some point, she was assigned to look into the background of one James Peabody in Cathcart, partly because she was from here. When I questioned her, she could hardly speak about him. The man she described was mean, petty and violent.

He'd abused her, viciously. She was left physically scarred and has never worked in the business since.

'Gail, she was no longer the same person. She was merely a shell of her former self. It was that incident that convinced me I needed to get the upper hand with the guy before we started dealing with him. So that's what I did. I'm sorry I didn't tell you what was going on, but I thought it might be better if you questioned him without any preconceived notions. Probably a bad call on my part, but there it is,' he fmished and sat back.

Connie and Gail looked at each other.

'Well,' Connie said finally, 'that certainly puts a different spin on things. Now what do we do?'

'I haven't a clue,' Gail said. 'And what in the world do you think was going on with Turner Redland? Is it possible he's had dealings with this character before and just isn't telling us everything he knows?'

Just then, Connie's cell phone buzzed. 'Hello,' he said.

'Hi, Connie. It's Turner.'

Connie put his phone on speaker before replying. 'I'm glad you called, Turner. I think we need to have another meeting, as soon as you can manage it.'

'Ah. So you've heard then,' Turner said. 'All hell's going to break loose now.'

'Heard *what*?' Connie looked at the others in concern. 'What the hell are you talking about, Turner?'

'I thought you meant . . . so you *haven't* heard then? Well, might as well tell you now. James Peabody's been found dead. His body was discovered earlier this morning.'

'Peabody dead?' Connie shook his head in disbelief. 'Come to the office as quickly as you can, Turner. You know the drill. Don't speak to anyone about this until we can decide what our next steps should be.'

Gail's phone was blinking now, too. 'Yes?' she said into the speaker. 'Who's calling, please?'

'Sam. It's Sam Weems, Gail. There's something you need to know.'

'I think I already know, Sam. Everything we discuss from now on must be off the record. But I remember the promise I made to you. And I'll make good on it.'

'I know you will, Gail. And there's something else about this you need to know as well. I can be over there in fifteen minutes, and the additional news I have is going to knock your socks off.'

'Join the crowd, Sam. See you at the office in fifteen minutes. All the usual suspects.'

Connie was already paying the bill and Hugo had gone on ahead to open up the office.

The game was afoot.

11

Ruth Moreland, still chilled from her bus ride into work, hurried in to the reading room, flipped the lights on, removed her top coat, and immediately began folding up yesterday's newspapers to get them ready for storage.

After taking down the paper from Cathcart, however, she took a seat at one of the patron's tables and carefully leafed through the whole thing page by page. She had been doing this each and every day since it had first occurred to her that having the Cathcart daily news disseminated to the citizens of Newton might not be in her best interest.

Finally, convinced there was nothing in yesterday's news that had anything to do with her prior existence, she folded up the paper and placed it with the others in the storage cabinet where they would remain until time to move them on to their next destination.

At some future date, all the hard copies of the local newspapers would be replaced with microfiche cards so that there would always be permanent records available for students and researchers. But that procedure was far beyond her present job classification and didn't concern her today.

Once yesterday's papers had been placed in the storage cabinet, she turned her attention to today's early-morning editions and began to drape them, one by one, over the rails as usual. When she got to *The Cathcart Sun*, however, she stopped short. Knees shaking, she picked up the paper, carried it over to a table and sat down again. Her hands were cold and her breath came in short bursts.

Carefully, she opened it up and laid it out on the work area in front of her. The morning headlines, outlined in crisp black ink, screamed out:

LOCAL MAN FOUND DEAD IN DESERTED HIDEAWAY

And then, immediately below, and in

slightly smaller type, the item she had been afraid of finding:

POLICE SEARCHING FOR DEAD MAN'S MISSING WIFE

A grainy I.D. photo from the Cathcart university archives stared back at her with unseeing eyes.

She clutched her chest and gasped out loud. The letters blurred and wavered in front of her. What were they talking about? Her last memory, when she fled the house that night, was of him sitting alone with the whiskey bottle in front of him. Had someone else come in later? But who could it have been? And, more importantly, *why was he killed?*

She shook herself back to reality. Hurriedly, she gathered up the rest of today's papers and spread them about on the rails, covering up *The Sun* as much as possible before fleeing out into the main area of the library.

Checking in at the reference desk, she found the librarian on duty. 'I'm so sorry,' she said, 'but I've got a terrible headache.

I think I might be coming down with something. I'm going to have to go home.'

'Oh, that's too bad,' said the woman. 'Do you want me to call anyone for you?'

'No. I'll be all right. I think I just need to lie down. Thanks.'

Clutching her tote bag, she ran out the front door of the Newton City Library and on to the bus stop.

She didn't know what she would do next. But one thing was certain. Ruth Moreland was no longer safe in Newton.

She'd have to go on the run again. And the sooner she left town, the better.

⋆　⋆　⋆

She got off the bus and scurried toward Mrs. Canty's boarding house, her mind whirling as she dashed down the street.

She stopped on the front porch to catch her breath and think. The other boarders were all out. She, Dora and Bill had all left for their city jobs this morning, right after breakfast. Joe, the

119

traveling salesman, was away on one of his regular rounds and wasn't expected back until much later in the day. That left Jack, the retired gentleman.

She smiled. Last night at dinner, Jack had mentioned he was planning to visit an old friend today, and that he would probably have his dinner out before he returned to the house.

She entered and paused to catch her breath in the still entry where pale winter sunlight dappled the carpet. Noises from the general area of the kitchen indicated that Mrs. Canty was beginning her meal preparations for the day.

She knocked on the door as she entered the kitchen, hoping not to startle the older woman. Mrs. Canty looked around in surprise.

'Why, Ruth, my dear,' she said. 'What are you doing home? Nothing wrong, is there?'

'Hello, Mrs. Canty,' she said. 'No, not really. I just have a terrible headache and didn't think I could stay and work any longer today. Sorry if I startled you.'

'Oh, that's a shame. You go on in and

sit down. Can I bring you something? A cup of tea?'

'No. Actually, I think I'm just going to go on up and lie down a bit. Maybe I can sleep it off.'

'That's right. You go take a nice long nap. I'll bring a tray up for you later on. Can I get you anything else? A hot water bottle? Do you have aspirin?'

'I'm fine. I'll be all right, I'm sure. I just need a little quiet time, I think.'

She turned to make her way out of the room and back to the entry to climb the stairs to her room. She paused a moment in the shadow of the doorway and watched Mrs. Canty get milk and eggs out of the refrigerator and place a large mixing bowl on the counter top.

Good. The older woman was making a pie or something. Her attention would be on that for a while. Maybe it would give Ruth enough time to do what she needed to do.

She darted up the stairs and down the hall, and unlocked her room door. Once inside, she thought a moment, then opened her closet, pulled out the backpack and began organizing its contents.

The most important things, of course, were her identification papers and the cash. She spread the latter between her handbag, a money belt which she strapped to her body beneath her slacks, and a zipper pocket hidden within the bowels of the backpack.

She decided to leave her nice work suit on, at least for now. She tucked as many tightly folded sets of clothing, mostly casual, into the crevices of the pack as would fit, and added a few small packets of toiletries. Then, after a moment of hesitation, she removed the pageboy wig from her head and tucked it in as well before zipping everything up.

Using her cell phone, she called a local cab and directed it to pick her up in fifteen minutes at an address halfway down the street from Mrs. Canty's house. She pulled her woolen top coat back on and stood in the middle of the room looking around at her erstwhile home. It was too bad she had paid so far ahead on this place. Money wasted. But that couldn't be helped now.

Satisfied with her arrangements at last, she tiptoed to the door and peeked out into the hallway. No one was in sight, and she thought she could hear Mrs. Canty down in the kitchen, humming a tune and clanging dishes and pots around.

She stepped out of the room, turned, and made her way down the darkened hall in the opposite direction. There was an old servants' stairway at the rear of the house that led directly to a utility area and the back door. Moving as quietly as possible, she reached the bottom of the stairs, waited a moment to make sure Mrs. Canty was well occupied, then slowly unlocked and opened the creaky old door leading out into the back yard.

She stepped onto the back stoop and let the screen door close softly behind her before creeping silently down the rickety wooden steps. Once in the overgrown back garden, she hefted her pack and headed around the house on the side opposite the kitchen to the front yard. After checking carefully to make sure no one, like a utility reader, was lurking about, Ruth hurried out the gate and down the street just as the cab pulled up at the neighboring location as she had requested.

The cabbie stowed her backpack in the trunk of the car and helped her into the back seat before swinging the fare meter back to zero. 'Where to, lady?' he said, pulling out into the street.

'The Eastside Shopping Center,' she said. 'The entrance on 3rd Avenue.'

'You got it,' he said. And the woman who had been Ruth Moreland was on her way to a new life.

* * *

The cabbie stopped right in front of the entrance to the mall. Ruth climbed out and waited for him to retrieve her pack from the trunk.

'Do you need some help with this, lady?' he said, eyeing the bulk of it and her nice suit.

'No, I'm fine,' she said, handing him the fare plus a small but reasonable tip. 'I'm used to carrying it.'

He shrugged, went around and climbed back into his cab, and sat there a minute, looking over his records and preparing for his next call.

Ruth entered the mall doorway but hung back in the shadows of the large overhang, waiting for the taxi to leave. At length the cabbie put away his journal, switched on his blinker and pulled out into traffic. Once he was out of sight, she stepped back out onto the sidewalk and hurried down the street in the direction of the bus depot.

This was the same station where she had disembarked from the Cathcart bus just a few short days ago, and she had the layout of the waiting room still in her mind when she entered the bustling building.

She immediately turned to her right and headed toward a bank of lockers where she fumbled with coins and deposited the backpack, safely out of the way and out of sight. She made her way back to the middle of the room and the main ticket counter. After waiting in line for what seemed like forever, she confronted the clerk.

'Yes?' he said. 'May I help you?'

'What time does the next bus to Los Angeles leave?' she said.

'Los Angeles?' The clerk straightened to attention. He didn't get many requests for L.A. 'Let me see.'

He pulled out a set of schedules and began perusing it, running a broad broken-nailed finger down the well-worn page.

'Yes, here it is. The only bus going out this afternoon is leaving in about 30 minutes. You can just catch it if you hurry. If you don't take this one, you'll have to wait until 3:30.'

'Fine. Give me a ticket.' She paid him in cash. 'Which gate is it?'

'It's Gate 5. You can just make it if you hurry.' He pointed to a doorway marked 'Gates 5–10.'

'Thank you,' she said, grabbing the ticket and running in the direction of the gate.

But as she neared it, she slowed and blended in with a group of chattering women obviously on a tour or attending a

126

conference together. One or two looked at her suspiciously, but she feigned indifference and joined in as if she belonged with them.

As the group fluttered its way across the waiting room, she suddenly veered off and away and quickly made her way back to the locker area.

Once there, she retrieved her pack and ducked into a nearby restroom where she found and entered an empty stall.

She stripped off her top coat, suit jacket and top and replaced them with a casual tee and quilted ski jacket out of the pack. She exchanged her dress pumps for tennis shoes, and finally, she pulled out the pageboy wig and fixed it to her head, cramming the knit cap down over it. She glanced in the mirror as she left the restroom.

The well-put-together woman in the stylish business suit, the one with the cropped grey hair who had entered the depot a short time ago and purchased a ticket to Los Angeles — that woman had vanished. The other woman, dressed casually, with the reddish-brown pageboy, was on her way to someplace else.

⋆   ⋆   ⋆

Choosing the doors near the front of the depot waiting room, she pushed through and out onto the cement passenger loading docks for Gates 1 through 4. A fusty, lingering exhaust odor permeated the area, and she wrinkled her nose in protest.

Beginning on the end closest to the street entrance, she began making her way slowly down the line, checking the lighted destination placards on the front of each bus waiting in line for departure.

Some had already started their engines, indicating they were within five minutes of leaving the station. Others, sitting in silence, had longer to wait for departure, so were observing the law prohibiting idling in an enclosed area for longer than five minutes.

She took her time. Some of the cities were only a few hundred miles from Newton and even Cathcart, and she deliberately passed them by without another thought. Other town names were unfamiliar to her, so she had no idea at all of where they were located.

At last, near the end of the line, and just as she was about to give up hope and turn back, she stopped short.

'Marshall,' blinked the lighted sign over the broad, fly-specked windshield.

Marshall, she knew, was a medium-sized town located near the hilly northeastern border of the state. It was at least a day's ride from Cathcart, and about as far away from Newton as you could get and still be in the same state.

As she stood there, the driver switched on the motor and began his five-minute countdown to departure. Without hesitation, she swung up and onto the bus through the still-open doors.

'Are you going to Marshall?' she said, knowing the answer to her question.

'Yes, ma'am. You got a ticket?'

'Is this still good?' She held out her intra-state bus pass, used most recently on her getaway from Cathcart to Newton.

He scanned it briefly. 'Yes, ma'am. It's

as good as gold. This bus is pretty full . . . ' He glanced up in the rear-view mirror. ' . . . but I think there may be a seat or two left in the back there. One way or round trip?'

'One way,' she said, breathing a sigh of relief. 'I don't know what day I'll be returning.'

He clipped the pass and handed it back to her. 'Better get seated,' he said. 'We're about ready to get going.'

Clutching her backpack, she joggled her way down the aisle, ready to grab the first vacant seat she spotted. She began to panic as she drew near the end of the bus, but smiled when the last row proved to be empty.

What luck! she thought to herself, plunking down near the window and hauling her pack in next to her. She even had the whole seat to herself!

She had to modify that thought a bit when a teenaged boy, smelling strongly of cigarette smoke and too much hair gel, pushed in beside her. But she had claimed the window seat, and that would have to do for now.

Tucking the clunky backpack in beside her next to the window, she settled down again and tried to make herself as comfortable as possible as the bus to Marshall slowly chugged out of Newton, leaving a trail of noxious fumes in its wake.

12

As her boarders began to drift in from work that afternoon, sniffing appreciatively at all the good smells emanating from the kitchen, Mrs. Canty started to wonder how Ruth was dealing with her headache.

Once she had her supper organized and her apple pie had come out of the oven and was cooling on the counter, she mentioned her concerns to Dora, who had just stomped in off the street in a huff.

'I don't *care* how she's doing,' Dora said. 'I had to go ask at the reference desk when she didn't show up for lunch. It was embarrassing, I want to tell you. She didn't even have the courtesy to let me know she was coming home early.'

'Now, now, Dora,' Mrs. Canty said, 'I don't think it was an intentional slight. She really wasn't feeling so good when she came in. She went right up to bed;

didn't even have a cup of tea or anything.'

'Well . . . ' Dora backed down a bit. 'Well, I still think it was rude of her. She could have asked them to let me know, at the very least. I ended up missing part of my lunch break because of it.'

'All the same,' Mrs. Canty said, 'I'm going to go on up and see if she needs anything. Maybe she'll feel up to coming down to supper.' And off she went before Dora could say anything else.

Personally, Mrs. Canty thought Dora was being just a bit mean-spirited about the affair. Ruth had been nothing but gracious and kind to everyone. Dora was just going have to get over her imagined slight.

She paused in front of Ruth's bedroom door, puzzled. It appeared to be slightly ajar. Surely Ruth would have closed it before retiring. She gave a tentative knock before pushing it open and peeking inside.

A few moments later, she rushed into the sitting area where the others were gathering to wait for their evening meal.

'She's gone!' Mrs. Canty said, breathing hard from her climb up and quick descent down the front stairs.

'Gone?' Bill stood up. 'What in the world do you mean? Who's gone?'

'Ruth. She came home earlier today with a splitting headache and went to her room to lie down. Now the door's wide open and she's not there. What's more, her bed hasn't been slept in at all. It's still just as I made it up this morning.'

Jack Williams, who had just come in from the afternoon out with his friend, stepped forward. 'Do you think she didn't go upstairs to her room after all?'

'She most certainly did,' Mrs. Canty said. 'At least that's what I thought, although I was busy in the kitchen when she came in. I offered her a cup of tea, which she turned down. She said she was going to go up and go straight to bed.'

Joe, who had just come in from his sales trip, immediately headed for the stairway. 'We need to check her room just to make sure nothing has happened to her. But how in the world could she have left the house without being noticed by someone?'

Led by Joe, the other boarders and Mrs. Canty all trooped upstairs together and into the room belonging to Ruth Moreland. The men stood back at first and let the women begin the search, out of respect for Ruth's privacy. But soon they were all searching through the space, seeking some explanation for her sudden departure.

Finally Jack, seated in the easy chair near the window, looked at the others, his face etched with worry. 'I think we'd better contact the police,' he said. 'Something doesn't feel quite right about this.'

Bill looked at Mrs. Canty in concern. 'You indicated earlier that she was paid ahead on her room. Is that really the case? Does she owe you any money at all?'

'No, she doesn't,' the older woman said emphatically. 'In fact, back in July she originally paid for the room for a year in advance. Of course, a small part of that was used up in July. But she still has almost a year left on the books. So no, she definitely doesn't owe *me* any money. I don't know about anyone else, of course . . . ' She looked around the room at the others.

Slowly, one by one, they each acknowledged that Ruth had not asked for a cent in loans from anyone. Even Dora admitted that Ruth had paid for her bus ride that very morning when she had come up short of change.

'So it doesn't appear to be a money issue,' said Bill. 'What about foul play? Does there seem to be any indication of that here?' He looked at the women, who had gone through Ruth's dresser and closet.

'No,' said Dora. 'Nothing seems out of place, exactly. But I'm sure there must be a few things missing. For instance, she mentioned she bought an expensive face cream because she was having dry skin issues. I don't see that anywhere in here, and I looked for it.'

'And her backpack,' Mrs. Canty said. 'She arrived carrying that huge backpack. It was heavy, I could tell, so there must have been a lot of things in it. Well, that's definitely gone. I looked through the whole closet pretty carefully. It's not there. And most of the clothes that she left are suited for work. All her casual things are gone.'

'O.K.,' Bill said, 'I think that's enough. I think you should lock this door, Mrs. Canty. And I think we should call the police and report this as a disappearance.'

'I agree,' said Joe. 'But one of the problems will be that we have no idea why she left. She's an adult, and she doesn't appear to have committed any crime. I doubt the police will do anything about it, at least not for a while. I don't know if it'll do any good to report her missing.'

'We have to at least try,' said Jack. He was pale and looking a bit ill. 'Maybe there's a waiting period before they'll start looking for her. But I think we have to make the attempt. This just doesn't feel right to me somehow.'

In the end, they took a straw vote and all agreed that Mrs. Canty would lock up Ruth Moreland's room and that they would, as a group, report her disappearance to the local authorities and let it go from there.

Dora also suggested she speak to the library administration the following day and then try to find out if Ruth had said anything to anyone there about her reasons for leaving.

'After all,' she said, 'no one gives up a paying job without a damn good reason, at least not in my book.'

13

Gail's assistant, Margaret, had just come in and was removing her coat when her boss dashed in and motioned her into the inner office.

'We're expecting visitors,' Gail said. 'Try to cancel any non-essential appointments for all of us, and alert the rest of the staff. We may be going into high gear now.'

'High gear' meant that a high-profile case or project was imminent, which would probably mean overtime and research assignments for all members of the firm.

'Do you want me to contact anyone else?' Margaret said. 'Mr. Walton or Mr. Powell?'

Gail hesitated. Charles Walton, their partner, was based in Phoenix, while Damon Powell, their former intern, now had a thriving practice of his own to maintain.

'Yes,' she said. 'But just give them a heads-up that we might be involved shortly in an extremely high-profile case. We might have to have all hands on deck before we're through. I don't think Mr. Walton needs to make travel plans just yet, but suggest to him he might want to start looking at clearing his calendar. Damon — Mr. Powell — is a different situation. Just tell him I'll call him today or later this evening and let him know what's going on.'

Margaret laid out yellow pads and pens then turned to the coffee station. 'The big pot?'

'Oh, yes, Margaret,' Gail said, sorting through the notes on her desk. 'Definitely put on the big pot today.'

Once the coffee was bubbling away, Margaret left the room just as Connie and Hugo entered and began pulling extra chairs in around the conference table. Gail paused and stared out at the grey sky.

'Looks like it might start to snow again,' she said. 'We'll certainly have appropriate weather for this.'

There was a knock on the door. It opened and Margaret ushered in Turner Redland. There was a little flurry while he removed his top coat and hung it near the heating vent to dry. He took his seat at the conference table, removed a thick file from his brief case, and was just opening it up when another knock came at the door.

Everyone looked up as Sam Weems entered. He, too, removed his coat and made his way to the table.

'Sam,' said Turner, nodding to him. 'This is a bit of a surprise.' He looked pointedly at Gail. 'You realize, of course, that everything we'll be discussing here today must be kept in the strictest confidence. We'll be off the record.'

Gail spoke up. 'He's aware of that, Turner. But I'm hoping Sam will have more information for us.'

'I'm prepared to respect your request for confidentiality,' Sam said. 'We haven't released anything yet in the paper, other than the bare facts of Peabody's death and the news about his missing wife. We haven't made any statement or drawn any conclusions about the blackmail attempt in connection with your office either. But you realize I won't be able to hold off on that information for very long.

'I've come prepared to give you everything the paper has thus far,' he went on. 'All I ask is that when you're prepared to make an official statement about the other matter, as I assume you will at some point, all I want in return is an exclusive about it. If you can give us that reassurance, then we'll cooperate in any way which is most helpful to the community.'

'I'm willing to take you at your word, Sam,' said Turner. He looked over at Gail. 'Do you think we need anything in writing from him?'

Gail paused. All her instincts and experience in the law said yes, but she had known Sam for many years now. He had been most helpful to her during her first big case. The fact was, she had never known him to do anything unethical. She made a decision.

'No,' she said. 'I think we can all agree here to keep this under wraps until we have a better handle on just what's happened.' She turned back to Sam. 'What do *you* know about Peabody's death? And what's this about his wife going missing? Just who is she? And do you think she could be involved?'

'Honestly? I have no idea. In fact, nobody seems to know just when she disappeared or why.' Sam turned to the D.A. 'I suspect you have more information on all that than I do at this point.'

'All we know about the case,' Turner said, 'is that some friend or colleague of Peabody's was supposed to meet him at his house. When he showed up, the door was standing open, which was out of character for Peabody. The friend entered and called out, and when there was no answer, he began searching the place. That was when he found Peabody's body in the den. He'd been seated at the desk and there was a bullet hole through his head. The gun used in the shooting was lying on the floor nearby.'

'Suicide?' Hugo said. 'Sounds classic.'

'Well, there were several anomalies, which I won't take the time to go into

143

here, that indicate it was more likely a homicide. In fact, I've prepared fact sheets for everyone with some of the forensic details we've uncovered thus far.' He pulled some papers from his file and passed them around the table to the others. 'Of course, we're in early days here. There'll be a lot more information, we hope, once the medical examiner finishes his report.'

'And what about Peabody's wife?' Connie said. 'How did you discover she was missing?'

'Once the authorities got there and took a statement from the friend, he told them Peabody was married, but he'd never met the woman, and he had no idea where she'd gone.'

'Seems odd,' said Hugo. 'What about the neighbors? They know anything?'

'The place is out in that area that borders on the National Forest. The neighbors are few and far apart, and James Peabody and his wife apparently kept to themselves. The people we were able to find in the area said they didn't really know either of them and had no idea where she might be. We began searching the house for clues and quickly discovered evidence that she is, or has been until recently, employed at the university. In fact, it appeared she wasn't even using Peabody as a surname. She was a professor by the name of Anne Cromwell, and she'd been teaching in the English department there for a number of years. When we contacted the university police, they confirmed she was employed there, but her department had her listed as on extended family leave, claiming she was caring for an ill family member in another state. They had no more information about her whereabouts than that.'

Gail thought a moment. 'I think I'll give Damon Powell and his wife a call,' she said. 'They both attended classes at the university. Maybe they'll remember something about her. Especially if she'd been employed there for a while.'

'That's a good idea,' said Connie. He turned to Redland. 'Do you have any objection to us bringing them in on the case?'

'If they can add anything to this puzzle,

I'm more than happy to have them on board,' the D.A. said.

'The other thing we found interesting when we searched the house,' Turner continued, 'is that Ms. Cromwell, wherever she's gone, didn't take her purse, her I.D., her checkbook, or any other personal items with her name on them. It looked as if she just walked out the door with nothing but the clothes on her back.'

'Is it possible she was kidnapped or otherwise harmed by the person who killed Peabody?' Hugo said. 'Maybe she's a victim, too.'

'We've considered that possibility. In fact, we've already put out an APB on her, even though as an adult, she can't be presumed to be missing for a certain period of time. The fact is, every cop in the state is now looking for her. And since we aren't even sure she's still *in* the state, it's going to be like looking for a needle in the proverbial haystack. The pictures we were able to access all look like any other Jane Doe. There's nothing unique about her, and she resembles any other nice-looking middle-aged lady professor.

It's going to be extremely difficult to track her down, especially if she's disguised herself in any way.'

Gail shook her head. 'At least one thing is sure,' she said. 'Poor old James Peabody isn't going to be blackmailing anyone else in the future.'

14

Ruth Moreland sat scrunched up against the window seat as the bus chugged along the highway, headed northeast and up into the hillier regions of the state.

At least now she was moving further away from both Newton and Cathcart. But she still had no idea what she was going to do once she reached Marshall. She had enough cash on her to pay for food and lodging for at least a while, so there she had no immediate worries about being forced onto the streets. Without a steady stream of income, however, that situation wouldn't last forever.

She would have to get into a safer situation, in some other state maybe, find a decent-paying job if at all possible, and work towards starting a new life.

She squeezed back tears, thinking about the many kindnesses of her fellow boarders and Mrs. Canty. Even though it had been difficult to live in disguise, as someone else, it had been far better than trying to survive in constant fear and abuse.

How had she gotten into this situation? If James Peabody really was dead, maybe she should just go back to Cathcart and turn herself in to the police. If the authorities found her now, living under an alias and on the run, it would go quite badly for her; she was certain of that.

She tried to think back to just before she left and review again everything that had happened. She had returned from work and started dinner. He'd come in a short time later in a bad mood, and began drinking again. Soon her dinner had gone uneaten and the house was a mess, smelling of whisky and half-smoked cigarettes. The inevitable heated argument over nothing in particular was followed by the violent confrontation which had led to her desperate getaway.

Had she dreamt that whole scenario and its aftermath? How had she gotten it all so wrong? And if she had known in advance what was to happen, would she still have fled the scene?

149

She shook her head. No matter how many times she reviewed everything that had occurred, she was certain she would not . . . could not . . . have done things any differently.

As she watched the changing landscape, the clouds darkened and rain began plummeting down, slanting towards her pinched face reflected in the bus window.

Soon night would fall and she would once again be a stranger in a strange land.

★ ★ ★

Four hours into the journey, the bus rumbled to a stop in front of a diner rest stop.

'Thirty minutes,' called out the driver. 'Don't take too much time. There's another storm brewing over the hills.'

The young man next to her stirred, stretched, and started to get up.

'Wait a minute,' she said. 'Do you want me to watch your pack for you? I'm not going in, but I'd appreciate it if you could bring me a sandwich or something.' She held out a $20 bill.

He looked at her in suspicion, then relented and took the money. 'What d'ya want?'

'Whatever you can find. I don't care,' she said. 'Get yourself something, too.'

He didn't say anything, but tucked the bill into the pocket of his jacket and hurried down the aisle.

She waited for what seemed like an eternity, thinking maybe she had made a mistake. But just before the driver started up the engine, indicating the five-minute idling period had begun, her seat companion pushed his way aboard and headed toward the back of the bus. He flung himself down, reeking of smoke, and handed her a small brown bag.

'Here,' he said. 'Hope that's O.K.'

'I'm sure it is,' she said. 'Thank you very much for doing this for me. I appreciate it.' She smiled in his direction.

He wiggled uncomfortably. He was unused to such attention, at least of the positive kind. 'That's all right,' he said. 'Thanks for the money, and for watchin' my bag.'

Clearly, this was not a situation he dealt with every day. She opened the paper bag, damp from the still-falling rain, and inspected its contents. Nestled inside were a ham and cheese sandwich wrapped in wax paper, a shiny red apple, and a small bag of chips. She glanced at him again. 'Thank you,' she repeated. 'This is perfect. It's just what I would have picked for myself.'

He looked at her in surprise. 'Oh, good,' he said. 'I tried . . . I tried to find somethin' you would like.'

He smiled back at her, settled back in his seat, and immediately fell asleep, a soft snore emanating from his gaping mouth.

She turned back toward the window as the bus slowly rumbled its way out of the graveled parking lot and back out on to the highway. The rain by now had turned to sleet, and the roadside was piled high with slush from this and previous storms. She took out the sandwich and was pleased to find it included mustard and a sliced pickle.

Amazing what small pleasures can do

for one's disposition, she thought, glancing at the sleeping boy beside her. *Bless him. He just made my day.*

She ate every bite of the tasty sandwich, relished the small bag of salty chips, and crunched down on the tart apple to finish off her improvised meal. Sated, she leaned back against her pack and gazed out at the landscape whizzing by. There was nothing there to see, really; just miles and miles of wet road and banked snow interspersed with spindly high-country pines.

Almost against her will, she shut her eyes and gradually fell into a stupor; not really sleep, but a world nonetheless, between reality and fantasy. The steady hum of the tires against the road and the rumble of the bus motor, punctuated by frequent grinding as the driver changed gears to accommodate the rising slopes, produced a hypnotizing effect.

She didn't know how long she had actually been asleep, but suddenly she awoke from her restless dreams, certain that something was terribly wrong.

She realized that they had reached the

summit of Mount Putnam, the tallest ridge of their trip, and were at the point of beginning the steep descent down the other side into a large empty valley floor below. The icy sleet had turned into a solid snowstorm. In fact, large heavy flakes of the stuff were quickly blanketing the road and the deserted countryside beyond.

The driver down-shifted again and pressed the accelerator, gripping the steering wheel with both hands. The bus tiptoed forward, slowly at first, then gathering speed as it began its downward progress.

She could sense immediately that they were going too fast for the road conditions. She didn't realize at first what was happening when the bus began sliding off the side of the road towards the precipice. But as she strained to see, the driver began jerking the steering wheel choppily from side to side, trying to desperately to correct the situation before it got out of control.

Then he did something no experienced driver on an icy road would ever do. He stomped on the brakes. Hard.

Immediately, the bus whined and continued its sideways slide in earnest. Those passengers who were awake and thus witnessing the phenomenon began screaming, some even standing up and clambering towards the aisle. Others continued sleeping peacefully.

Ruth Moreland glanced at the dozing boy next to her. He was snoring away, mouth open, a thin strand of spittle trailing down toward his chin. Should she wake him up and alert him to their precarious situation? Or should she just let him remain asleep and blissfully unaware of their danger?

'Wake up!' she said, shaking him out of his stupor. 'We're going to have an accident, I think. A bad one. We need to get prepared for it.'

He sat up in confusion, looked around to get his bearings, and caught her eye. 'What's wrong?'

'The bus is sliding off the road,' she said as quietly and calmly as she could. 'I think we may be going over the side of the hill.'

Ashen-faced, he grabbed her hand and looked past her through the window. 'I think you're right,' he said, after assessing the situation. 'What are we gonna do?'

She made a quick decision. 'We're going to stick together and help each other,' she said firmly. 'We're going to hold on to our packs and each other ... and we're going to survive. That's what we're going to do.'

Just as her words were uttered, the bus gave a final mighty lurch and the driver was thrown from his seat into the aisle, as were all those passengers foolish enough to be caught standing up at the moment of impact.

Ruth's forehead was flung violently against the window pane, rendering her unconscious. Her final vision before blackness overcame her, as the bus slid over the side of the mountain, through the spindly trees and onto a snowy bluff below, was of Mrs. Canty pulling a spicy apple pie out of the oven and placing it on her kitchen counter to cool.

'There, there, dear,' she heard the older

woman say, patting her hand. 'Everything's going to be all right now.'

★   ★   ★

She came to with a splitting headache. She had no idea how long she had been unconscious, but she didn't think it could have been longer than a few moments, given the still-spinning bus wheel she could barely glimpse out the window, and the scattered state of her fellow passengers and their belongings.

Smoke appeared to be rising from under the crumpled bus chassis, and she couldn't see far enough through the mess blocking the aisle to determine if the driver was still at the front, or if he had abandoned his post to join the chaos of humanity attempting to save itself from a possible explosion and fire.

She felt a tentative poke on her shoulder and turned to see her seat companion, now even more disheveled than in his normal state, trying to get her attention.

'C'mon,' he yelled above the fray. 'We

gotta get the hell outta here — now!'

He shouldered his pack and reached over to pull hers away from the crumpled window.

'Do you think you can carry this and still walk all right?' he said doubtfully, helping her into the straps.

She nodded, numb, her head still splitting with pain. No matter what, she must hold on to her backpack. It contained her whole world.

'How . . . ?' she began, still disoriented, as he half-pulled, half-pushed her up and out of their row and into the smoke-filled aisle.

'No time for that. It's gonna blow for sure,' he yelled in her ear. 'There's a side door halfway up the aisle. I'm gonna try to reach it. Here,' he added, guiding her hand through his backpack strap, 'hang on to me.'

Through pure determination, the pair dragged themselves up the aisle to the midway portion where the bus had split nearly in two. There were a few passengers struggling with the side door, but it remained stubbornly jammed shut.

'Here, let me,' he said, shouldering them aside. He grabbed a loose arm rail from one of the seats and began attacking the door seam with brute force. One of the men stepped forward and began to help, banging on it with his briefcase.

Suddenly, with a whoosh, the door burst open. The half dozen passengers who had gathered nearby pushed through. They stood back, his arm guarding her from joining them.

'Let them go,' he said. 'Let them all get out and go first. Then we can sneak through and get away down the hill.'

She looked at him in sudden realization. He must be on the run, too! He didn't want to be found and interrogated by the authorities any more than she did.

'Fine,' she said. 'Do you know a way out of here? Down into the valley and on into Marshall, I mean?'

'Yeah,' he said. 'I grew up here. If you want to throw in with me, I can get us out of here.'

The doorway finally cleared and they gingerly edged through. Outside, people were stumbling around in a daze. The driver was nowhere to be seen. She supposed emergency crews had been called from survivors' cell phones, but she had no idea how long ago, or how long it would take for help to arrive.

The two scrambled down the slippery steps out of the bus and through the gathering smoke. He quickly guided her to a snowbank at the edge of the bluff, where they struggled up and over the top and rolled down into a copse of trees hidden from the turmoil above them.

'This way,' he commanded, leading her further on down the hill.

Blindly, she followed him, either into salvation or into oblivion. And truth be known, she no longer cared which one it was.

15

Mrs. Canty and most of her boarders were gathered in the sitting room, awaiting the arrival of the police detective who had reluctantly agreed to come out and speak with them about the strange disappearance of Ruth Moreland.

The only one missing from their little group was Dora Dunn. She had yet to come in from the library. Either the bus was running late, or she had stopped for some unknown reason to take care of an errand.

Mrs. Canty sighed. They had planned this meeting so carefully . . . and now to have one of the more important members of the group not show up in time. She herself had spent most of the morning cleaning, dusting, vacuuming the carpet and fluffing up the pillows in the sitting room. She had even baked an apple pie, knowing that its spicy fragrance would permeate the whole house with a pleasant aroma. They could have it for supper tonight, along with the pot roast simmering away in the oven, she thought. At least that much was done.

Jack Williams, the older retired man, was looking a bit peaked. She hoped the stress of all this wasn't going to be too much for him.

The other two, Joe the salesman, and Bill the bank teller, were in fine form, however, comparing notes about Ruth's disappearance and the best way to present it to the detective, when he arrived.

The doorbell rang and they all looked up in expectation.

'Do you want me to get it?' asked Bill.

'No, that's all right,' Mrs. Canty said, rising out of her favorite chair. 'I think it's better if I go.'

She made her way through the room and into the entryway. There was a shadowy outline behind the etched pane of antique mica glass. Taking a deep breath, she opened the front door and confronted the person on the other side.

'Mrs . . . Canty?' said the man standing on the porch.

'Yes,' she said. He was dressed in plain clothes, something she had not expected. 'Are you . . . ?'

'I'm Detective Greenaway,' he said. 'Hank Greenaway. I understand you wish to make a missing person report?'

'Come in, please,' she said, and stood back to allow him to enter. 'Do you want to leave your coat?' She indicated the front hall tree.

'Thank you,' he said, pulling off his top coat. He scraped his feet on the mat. 'Sorry . . . '

'No, that's all right. We're used to the rain and snow. Come right along into the sitting room. We're all . . . well, most of us . . . are in there.'

He took an appreciative sniff. 'Smells like you've been baking,' he said. 'Nice.'

'Well, it's just pie, but maybe you'd like a piece after we've finished . . . ?'

He smiled. 'Well, let's just see how long this takes. I don't want to keep you from your routine.'

They moved into the sitting room,

where the men all rose as they were introduced to Greenaway, and he to them.

'Now,' he said, taking the seat near the side table Mrs. Canty indicated to him, 'let's get down to business. Who's gone missing, and why do you think the police should be involved?'

Bill Wallace took the lead. Considering his notes, he carefully went over Ruth Moreland's history as far as they knew it, followed by a summary of her recent return to the boarding house, the new job, and her sudden disappearance from their midst.

'You see, sir,' he said, 'it just doesn't seem like something she'd do — leave like that without saying goodbye or giving some explanation for it. That's the part that seems disturbing.'

Henry Greenaway had been taking notes of his own. He had the situation pretty well sized up, but he didn't want to offend these people. They all seemed like nice individuals who were simply concerned about someone whom they really didn't know very well. It had already

164

occurred to him that Ruth Moreland, or whatever her name was, had been holed up here for a day or two just as a matter of convenience. Then something had happened, or she had gotten unexpected information of some kind that had convinced her to hit the road again and move on with her life.

'Was she close to any one of you, more than the others, for instance?' he said. 'Is there something she may have said to any of you that might give us a clue as to why she would have made this sudden decision?'

There was silence for a moment. Then Mrs. Canty spoke up. 'Well,' she said. 'There's Dora.'

'And who's Dora?' he said, puzzled.

'She was supposed to be here with us. She boards here, too.' Joe sounded disgusted.

Dora had been the main one wanting to bring the police into it. If she didn't show up now, while the detective was here, they would all look like fools.

'And why do you think she might have additional information?'

165

Greenaway was beginning to tire of this assignment. The boarders were probably just a bunch of busybodies with too much time on their hands, making up mysteries where none actually existed.

'Well,' Mrs. Canty said, 'she and Ruth were friends of sorts, I guess. Dora had gotten Ruth her job at the library, in fact. They took the bus in together this morning, and I fixed their lunches for them so they could eat together. I guess if Ruth had confided in anyone, it would have been Dora.'

Greenaway sighed. 'Well, it's too bad she isn't here, if she did have additional information. The problem is, unless there's some sign of criminal activity or that violence has occurred, Ms. Moreland is an adult and has every right to come and go as she pleases. Without any other indication that she left under duress or has committed any crime . . . '

At that very moment they heard the front door loudly open and slam shut, followed by stomping feet down the hall to the sitting room. They all looked up to see Dora Dunn standing in the doorway, red-faced and heaving, still wearing her rain-damp coat with a knitted cap jammed down on her head.

'I've got news!' she announced, looking around at them wild-eyed. 'It's about Ruth . . . and you're not going to believe it!'

16

'So what's your name?' Ruth asked as the two trudged along.

He looked at her. 'Do you think that's a good idea?'

'Well, we don't have to use our real names, I suppose,' she said. 'But it would be more convenient to have something other than 'Hey, you' to get your attention.'

'What's *your* name then?' he said, putting the burden back on her.

She paused and thought about it. She didn't want him to know her real name any more than he wanted her to know his.

'Frances,' she said. Frances Long, the H.R. lady at the library, had been more than kind to her. Why not honor her in some small way. 'You can call me Frances.'

'Okay, *Frances*. And you can call me Jésus.' He put an accent on the first syllable, as any Latino would.

'All right, *Hey*-sus it is,' she said. 'How far away is Marshall now, do you think? I don't know how much further I can walk.'

'Not going to Marshall . . . '

Her heart sank. Had he led her into a trap? Where in God's name was he taking her?

He noticed her discomfort. 'Don't worry, Frances,' he said. 'I'm not leading you astray. It's way too far for us to walk all the way in to Marshall. Besides, it would be the middle of the night by the time we got there. That wouldn't be so good. No. If I've got my bearings right, we'll be safe very soon now. Just you wait and see.'

He said nothing further until they had reached the top of the next hill, where he turned to her excitedly. 'There it is!' he said. 'It's just as I remembered it. We'll be okay now.'

So saying, he turned and began rapidly run-walking down the slope toward what looked to be a small ramshackle shed in a clearing just beyond a cluster of under-growth.

She followed a little slower. She was bone-tired and her head still ached. What in the world was he thinking? The place he was running toward looked like nothing more than an old grey-shingled doghouse.

As they grew closer, however, she could see the outline of the place a little better. It was actually a rough hunter's cabin with a rickety wooden porch running across the front. They climbed unsteady steps up to the door, which was secured by a sturdy hasp and padlock. The boy seemed taken aback for a minute.

'I forgot Gramps kept a lock on it,' he said. 'I'll have to try and break it open somehow.'

'Wait a minute,' she said. The whole situation was reminiscent of the first night she'd spent in the hay shed. She put her pack down and felt in one side. Yes! It was still there!

She took out the small tool kit and handed it to him. Pulling out the lanyard under her shirt, she switched on the tiny light at the end of her key fob and held it steady while he worked away at the rusty screws holding the hasp. Ever so slowly, one, then another, began to turn.

Finally the lock fell away and Jésus threw the door open. Frances cast her small light into the darkness beyond. 'Here,' he said, pointing towards the back wall. 'There should be a candle some-where.'

Soon one was found and lit from the boy's cigarette lighter. They looked around and took stock of their surround-ings.

The cabin consisted of one large room with a few rudimentary pieces of furniture and dominated by a central stone fireplace. A counter across one wall appeared to hold cooking utensils.

'It's not much,' he admitted. 'But it's as sound as Gramps could make it. We should be able to get some rest before heading out for Marshall in the morning.' He gestured toward an old army cot in one comer. 'You take that. I'll roll up some blankets on the floor. I'm going to try to start a fire.'

By some miracle, dry wood was already laid in the fireplace and they discovered kitchen matches in a jar on the mantel. Soon there was a warm fire blazing away.

She cuddled up with her pack on the cot and fell asleep almost immediately. *Truly*, she thought as she drifted off, *truly, Jésus is my savior.*

★ ★ ★

When she woke the next morning, the fire had gone out and Jésus was nowhere to be seen.

So much for my savior, she thought bitterly, checking to make sure her backpack was still strapped securely to her wrist and had not been tampered with. *He's done a runner and left me out here in the wilderness to fend for myself.*

She took back the thought immediately when the door banged open and the boy trudged in bearing a load of firewood salvaged from under the porch overhang. 'Outhouse is just off the stoop and to the back,' he said, gesturing with his thumb after depositing the load of wood. 'I'll get the fire started up again.'

She gingerly climbed off the cot and

made her way to the door, still clinging to the backpack.

'You can leave that here if you want,' he said. 'I won't bother it.'

She hesitated just a moment before deciding to risk it. 'Thanks,' she said, leaving it on the cot. 'I won't be long.'

She struggled a bit, making her way out to the tiny privy at the back of the shed. While there, she thought about her situation. Obviously, she needed to convince Jésus that it was necessary for them to get into Marshall as quickly as they could.

'The sooner we can get there and get settled,' she said to him when she came back in a few minutes later, 'the less chance there will be the authorities will find us; that is, if they're even looking for us at all. After all, we have no idea what happened after we left the bus. It could have blown up, for all we know. If so, the passenger records might have been destroyed along with it. And what did they know about us, anyway?'

He nodded. 'Sounds good to me,' he said. 'But it's quite a hike into Marshall from here. Do you think you're up for it?'

She touched her sore head. She had taken a couple of aspirin from the stash in her pack before going to sleep. It felt better, but she had no idea if she had suffered a concussion with the blow. Other than that, she seemed all right, beyond sore muscles from her exertions of the previous day.

'I'm as ready as I'll ever be,' she said. 'If we can get into town and get rooms and a decent meal, at least we can rest for a while before taking stock and seeing what we need to do next.'

He looked at her and shook his head.

'I don't know what *I'll* do,' he said. 'Truth is, I'm all tapped out. I might be able to get a job washing dishes or somethin'. But that's not gonna pay much. I'm not even sure I can get a room on that.'

She thought a moment. 'What about this place? Who owns it now? Is your grandfather still alive?'

'Nope. Gramps died nearly a year ago. The place is supposed to be mine, but I don't have any money for food or nothin'.

I got a deed or somethin' that says its mine. But I'm not sure about that. Nobody ever explained none of it to me.'

'Do you mind showing it to me?'

He responded by rooting around in his own pack and pulling out a smudged and well-creased piece of paper. 'Here. This is what they gave me after Gramps died. I didn't know what to do with it, so I just stuck it away. I don't know if it's any good or not. Do you think it means I could live here? All the time, I mean?'

She took the page and carefully smoothed it out. Holding it so she could see it by the light of the candle he had lit, she studied it carefully.

'This is a land deed,' she said finally. 'It looks to me to be valid — that is, real. And it also looks to me as if it was signed over to you at the time of your grandfather's death and recorded in the Hall of Records. As far as I can tell, you own this place lock, stock and barrel. I see no reason why you couldn't stay here as long as you need.'

Neither of them stated the obvious — that she now knew his real name, which was recorded on the deed. It didn't seem to matter anymore.

He turned away from her suddenly, and she realized he was trying to hold back tears. 'Now,' she went on in a business-like tone to allow him to recover, 'the first thing you must do is find out if there are any taxes owing on the property.'

'Taxes? I can't pay no taxes.'

'Well, it might not be that much. But I can help you find all that out. The important thing is that you take advantage of this opportunity. Owning land is one of the best ways to become independent. Tto be your own person. To take control of your own life.'

'*Will* you help me?' he said. 'I mean, will you help me find out about all this?'

'I will help as much as I can,' she said. 'But I must tell you . . . ' She paused, suddenly in a panic. 'I *must* tell you that, just as you've probably suspected, I'm wanted by the police. It's a very serious charge. And I don't want . . . I can't . . . drag you into my problems. If I can stay undercover for a little while, I can at least find out about the taxes, and I can help you get set up. You know you're going to have to get a job?'

'I already figured on that. Look,' he went on, 'I don't want to put you in trouble with the law. You've been nothin' but kind to me.'

'And you very likely have saved my life,' she said. 'We still don't know what happened to that bus. If it blew up, there may be no record of me ever having been on it. And I doubt they'll be looking for me in Marshall yet, at least not right away.'

She closed her eyes as a sudden spasm of fear overcame her.

'Let's go on into Marshall and check on your taxes. That'll be a start at least. The most important thing now is that you secure your rights to this property. That gives you a stake in something at least.'

And if Marshall is the end of the road for me, then so be it, she thought, continuing to peruse the deed, marveling at the real name of the young man revealed to her there.

★   ★   ★

He put out the fire, then they made a final search of the cabin to make sure they hadn't forgotten anything before they strapped on their backpacks and headed out the door. She held it shut as he screwed the hasp back in securely. It wouldn't keep out determined intruders, but at least the interior would be protected from wildlife and the elements.

He continued down the slope and she struggled along in his wake. Her head still hurt, but she thought it might be getting better. All of her muscles ached from the unfamiliar exercise, but she was determined to keep up with him if at all possible.

He stopped at the bottom of the hill and waited for her to catch up. 'How ya doin'?' he said. 'It's still quite a way into town. Do you think you're gonna make it?'

She bent over, catching her breath and rubbing a stitch in her side. 'I'm not ready to stop yet. I'll go on as far as I possibly can.'

He looked at her doubtfully. He was beginning to wonder at the wisdom of this venture. Maybe she should have stayed behind, safe in the cabin, while he went into Marshall to get help.

'All right,' he said, 'let's keep on. Just let me know if you need to stop. We don't need to set any speed records.'

She didn't say anything, but gamely shouldered her pack and continued to follow him along what now seemed to be something of a game trail. The snow was not very deep here, but it was enough of a barrier that she had to force her steps forward with every ounce of strength she had left. He gradually pulled ahead of her until she finally lost sight of him around a bend in the path. She could see his footprints, however, and continued to follow them as best she could.

Suddenly, as she turned the bend, there he was in front of her, a big grin on his face. 'C'mon!' he said. 'We've broken through to the highway. It'll be easier goin' now.'

She looked beyond him and saw that the narrow trail they had been following had come to an end. Looking beyond, across what appeared to be a small field, was a much broader tarmac road heading northeast.

There were no cars on the road, but not far from where they stood, a large pickup with a snow plow hooked onto the front bumper was chugging along, throwing up a shower of snow and ice particles to either side and leaving a swath of open roadway in its path.

'That'll be Tomás — Tom, as most folks call him,' he said. 'Looks like he's been sent out from town to get the highway open. That's gonna help a lot.'

He broke into an ungainly lope across the field, hollering out at the top of his voice, 'Tomás, *Tom*. Hey, man. Wait up a minute!'

Miraculously, from that distance and over the rumble of the pickup motor, the driver inside the cab appeared to hear, or at least take notice of, the boy stumbling toward him. He stopped and waited, motor idling, until Jésus got nearer, before jumping down out of his perch and hailing the younger man. Ruth could just barely hear their exchange as she drew closer to the rig.

'*Hola,*' said Tom. '*¿Como 'sta?*'

'*Bien,*' said Jésus. '*¿Y usted?*'

'Aw, I'm okay, I guess. Can't complain. What you doin' way out here, boy? In the middle of all this snow and all?'

He turned a curious glance toward Ruth. 'And who might this pretty young thing be?'

Jésus didn't blink an eye. 'This is my Auntie Fran, on my mom's side,' he said easily. 'We were just checkin' out Gramps' old cabin up there when the blizzard hit. We're on our way back in to Marshall.'

'Hmmm,' said Tom. 'Well, you still got quite a way to go, folks.' He sized up the woman. 'If you don't mind ridin' in this ol' truck of mine, I can run you on into town.'

'Wouldn't want to take you away from your job and all,' said Jésus.

'*No hay problema,*' the older man said. 'I was just about to break off for lunch anyway. Come on. Hop in and hold on. Some of them bumps can be pretty bad.'

The two men helped Ruth up into the pickup cab. She didn't even object when

181

Jésus took her backpack and stored it behind the seat.

Tomás raised the plow blade and headed back up the road toward town, bouncing along over the drifts and berms.

She closed her eyes and savored the warmth of the truck heater and the fact that she was no longer hiking through the snow. What next? Would her name and picture be plastered all over Marshall when they got there?

She had no idea how long she would be able to keep up this charade.

★   ★   ★

It didn't take long for Tomás to negotiate the road heading in from the wilderness to downtown Marshall. As they bumped along, he kept up a string of conversation with the boy.

'You guys hear about that big bus wreck up on the interstate?' he said. 'Sounds pretty bad.'

'Nah,' Jésus said casually. 'We've just been at the cabin, lookin' things over and all, makin' sure everything weathered the storm all right.'

'Finally blew,' the older man said. 'Gas tank, I guess. I think there were some casualties. I imagine the authorities are gonna be goin' over that wreck pretty thorough like, makin' sure it wasn't caused by terrorists. You know how they are 'bout stuff like that these days.'

Jésus nodded. 'Guess so,' he said. 'I got no idea, really.'

'Well, good thing *you* weren't on it, right?'

Jésus didn't respond and Tomás turned his attention back to the road.

'Here we are,' he said after a bit. 'Good old town of Marshall. Where you guys want me to drop you off?'

'Any place is fine,' said Jésus. 'Don't want to take you out of your way.'

'Marshall's a pretty big area,' the older man said. 'I ain't gonna dump you guys off on the outskirts. Not after gettin' you this far.' He thought a moment. 'How 'bout I drop you over by the Donut Hole?' he said. 'That's not too far from the center of town, and at least you can

183

get a cuppa there; warm yourselves up a bit.'

'Sounds O.K.' Jésus sat back in his seat. 'Haven't been in there for a while. Still the same crew?'

'You talkin' 'bout Sheri? Last I heard, she's still there. Still single, too.' He looked over at the younger man and grinned. 'Maybe she's still pinin' for the old days, huh? What d'ya think?'

Jésus shifted uncomfortably. 'Nothin',' he said sourly. 'I don't think nothin' at all 'bout any of that.'

Ruth spoke up. 'Could I buy you something to eat, Tom?' she said. 'Or at least a cup of coffee; repay you for your kindness?'

'Aw, naw, ma'am,' Tom said. 'Not right now. I'm due back at the house. The wife will be waitin' on me for lunch and I'll have all he . . . heck . . . to pay if I don't get in on time.

'Maybe I'll see you around,' he added. 'You plannin' on stayin' in Marshall long?'

'No,' she said. 'I've got to get back home pretty soon. I just wanted to check on Jé . . . on Juan . . . just to make sure he was doing all right.' She coughed as if she had gotten something stuck in her throat. She had caught herself just in time, she hoped. This man would not know her companion as Jésus. He would only be known in these parts as Juan, the name she had seen on the deed.

Nothing more was said until they reached a bustling intersection which looked to be near the center of town. Tom pulled into a graveled parking lot adjacent to a diner with a big flickering neon sign out front proclaiming this to be 'The Donut Hole.'

He stopped and waited, motor idling, as they climbed down from the cab and pulled out their backpacks.

'Thanks, again, Tom,' the younger man said.

'Yes, thanks, Tom,' she echoed.

Tom regarded her thoughtfully. She wondered what he might be thinking, but had no crystal ball in her hand.

'All right, then,' he said, revving up the motor. 'You all take care, y'hear?'

And with a sputter of heavy duty tires

185

against wet gravel, Tomás chugged out of the parking lot and back onto the main thoroughfare.

17

Hank Greenaway sighed and got out his notebook again. At the very least, he would need to get this new person's story. Just more claptrap, he supposed.

Mrs. Canty brought Dora into the room, took her hat and coat, and motioned her to a chair near the heater. Once she was settled, the detective introduced himself and took down her full name.

'Now, Ms. Dunn,' he said, 'let me get this straight. You say you've discovered some brand-new information about Ms. Moreland's disappearance?'

'Yes, I have,' she said, emphasizing her words with a vigorous nod of the head. 'You all aren't going to *believe* what I found out this morning!'

They all stared at her in fascination. Dora was a known quantity in the boarding house. No one had ever mistaken her for a genius. And yet here

187

she was, proclaiming that she and she alone had figured out something that the rest of them, including the police detective, couldn't.

'Why don't you start at the beginning,' Greenaway said. 'Just where and when did you make this discovery?'

'Well . . . ' She settled in to tell her story. 'Well, I went in to work this morning, just as usual. I thought I could ask around in the library. You know, the people she — Ruth — had been working with yesterday.'

'About what time was this?' Greenaway asked, starting a new page in his notebook under 'Dunn, Dora.'

'It was shortly after I got in, maybe 8:30 a.m. or so. First I got myself a cup of coffee and thought about how to approach people without giving away that she — Ruth, I mean — had disappeared. The main ones I asked were the people she'd been working with at the reference desk. They weren't very helpful, except for the one she had told she was coming home.'

'And what was her name? Do you recall?'

'That was Isabel Klein.' She slowly spelled it out for him as he carefully wrote it down.

'And what explanation had Ms. Moreland given to Ms. Klein?'

'Well, as near as I can tell, it was the exact same story she gave Mrs. Canty here; that she had a splitting headache and was going to have to come home. She said she just couldn't work anymore that day.'

'And what time exactly did Ms. Moreland report that she was leaving the library to Ms. Klein?'

Dora looked confused. 'Now that, that's something I didn't think to ask Isabel. But I do know it was sometime before noon. Because that's when I began looking for her to go to lunch. She was gone before then.'

Greenaway turned to Mrs. Canty. 'And do you recall just what time she came in from work that day?'

Mrs. Canty closed her eyes. 'Let me see. I was in the kitchen . . . it was just as I was getting ready to put something in the oven. Seems to me it was about 10:30

or so, maybe a little earlier. Sorry I can't be any surer than that.'

'It's all right. Sounds like that allows enough time for her bus ride home. I just want to be sure she didn't stop off somewhere else along the way.' He turned back to Dora. 'Now, suppose you tell us what you discovered next?'

'Well, after I talked to Isabel, and got that part straight, I decided to backtrack to where she'd been working just before she left. I remembered she'd recently been assigned to the reading room to look after the magazines and newspapers in there on a regular basis.'

'So this was a new task she'd been given?'

'Yes. She told me about herself. She was really enjoying it, off on her own first thing in the morning, putting out the latest newspapers and such.'

Dora hesitated; then it all came out in a rush. 'And *that's* where I saw it!' Her voice went up a notch.

'Saw *what*?' Greenaway was getting impatient now. What in the world did this idiotic woman think she had seen, the face of Jésus on the windowpane?

'The newspaper.' Dora reached for her tote bag. 'I brought it with me,' she said. 'I thought it was important enough that we should all look at it together, to decide if I'm right or not.'

Carefully, she pulled out a folded newspaper and held it out to the detective. He opened it up and examined the first page for a moment or two before handing it over without comment to Mrs. Canty, as the others gathered around to look over her shoulder.

'Well,' he said after a minute to no one in particular, 'is that her?'

There on the first page of *The Cathcart Sun* was a spotty black-and-white photograph of a middle-aged woman. It looked like either an identification snap or even a mug shot. She was not smiling, but was staring straight ahead into the camera. The headline beneath read:

APB FOR MISSING WOMAN
WANTED FOR QUESTIONING
IN CONNECTION WITH
PEABODY MURDER

Mrs. Canty fell back in her chair. Jack Williams took the paper in his shaking hands.

'How can this be?' he said. 'Is this really her?'

'Look at it,' said Dora, triumph in her voice. 'Is there any doubt? It looks just like her — without the longer hair, of course. I always thought that was a wig. It looked too perfect.'

Bill Wallace took the paper next. 'Did you read this story? It says here that she was working at the university over in Cathcart as a professor.' He shook his head in wonderment. 'Who would have guessed?'

Joe grunted. 'Always thought she was a little too big for her britches,' he said. 'Always lordin' it over everybody.'

'Now don't you say that, Joe,' said Mrs. Canty. 'We don't know at all that this is her. They say everyone has a twin. Maybe this woman just looks like her. What we *do* know is that the Ruth Moreland who lived here with us was always kind and good-hearted. We need to remember that.'

Hank Greenaway sat there deep in thought as the voices rose and fell around him.

Damn! This was going to mess up the rest of his week; maybe even the weekend, too. Too bad he hadn't made his getaway before that Dumb Dora entered the scene with her earthshaking news.

★ ★ ★

The boarders and Mrs. Canty sat in stunned silence after Detective Greenaway took what evidence he'd been able to gather and left them to head back to his office.

'Now, don't none of you go up and go through her room anymore,' he had warned them. 'I'm sure we're going to have to send in a team of forensics specialists to see what they can find in the way of fingerprints and DNA samples. We'll probably have to have samples from all of you, too, since you've had access to her things.'

'You don't suspect any of us of aiding and abetting her, do you?' Bill Wallace had been horror-struck at the thought that his job at the bank might come into question.

'Oh, no,' Greenaway said. 'But I will expect you all to cooperate as much as possible with any investigation. And after all,' he added as he stepped out onto the porch, 'you did call *me* about this, remember?'

18

Jésus led their way into the diner and straight to a secluded booth at the back. They were met with a blast of warm air and the aroma of freshly brewed coffee.

She flung her pack in ahead and plunked down on the vinyl-covered bench. 'That coffee sure smells good,' she said. 'Do they serve anything besides donuts?'

'Yeah, they have pretty good food in here. At least they used to.' He looked around. 'I haven't been in here for a while.'

'Hi-ya, stranger,' came a voice at his side. 'What are you doin' back in town?'

The speaker was a young woman about the same age as Jésus. She was poured into a cheap white waitress's uniform covered with a wispy black apron. Her dark hair was pulled up in a bun with a pencil stuck through it. She turned over their mugs and filled them up with steaming black coffee.

'Hi, Sheri,' Jésus said, brightening up a little. 'You still knockin' 'round here?'

'Nothin' better to do,' she said. 'Can I getcha somethin' to eat? You and your . . . friend?' She glanced at the older woman skeptically.

'This here's my Aunt Fran,' he said. He looked across the table at her. 'Do you want somethin' to eat?'

Ruth smiled at the waitress. 'Hi,' she said. 'Do you serve hamburgers here? A hamburger with everything on it sounds great to me.'

'Yes, ma'am, we sure do, and they're the best burgers in town.'

'Fine. We'll take two of them with all the trimmings, and fries too, if you have them. And keep the coffee coming.'

Sheri wrote down their orders, stuck the pencil back in her bun and went back behind the counter, where she deposited their ticket with the cook. He plunked a couple of meat patties down on the grill with a sizzle.

'So that's Sheri,' she said. 'She looks like a nice young woman to me. You could probably do worse.'

'She's lookin' for somethin' I can't give her,' he said, resentment crowding his voice.

'Really? But as we've just discovered, you're a property owner now. And I'm pretty sure you can parlay that into something even more substantial, if you're just willing to take the chance.'

He shrugged and looked out the window. 'Nobody is much interested in someone like me,' he said. 'I've got no past and no future, and not a hell of a lot of hope of changin' that any time soon.'

'There's always hope, Juan,' she said, amazed at her own optimism. 'Never give up hope. If you do, you might as well be dead.'

They both sat there, sipping their coffee, and pondering her words until Sheri brought them the most delicious hamburgers either of them had ever eaten in all their lives.

Maybe hope is just a decent hamburger in a warm diner, she thought. *Maybe hope is really just what is around the next bend in the road. Maybe . . . just maybe*

. . . you are your own best hope after all.

As they ate, they went over what they should do next.

'We need to get rooms, cheap ones, in some place not too noticeable,' Ruth said.

'I can't keep taking money from you like this.' He shook his head. 'Usually, I'm the first one to take advantage. But you've been so good to me. I don't want to play that game with you.'

'And you got me off that bus and to your Gramps' place. And you spotted Tom and got us into town,' she said. 'I owe you much more than a meal and a room. I'll let you know when I don't think I can go any further.'

He thought a moment. 'There's a rooming house right up the street from here. Sheri's grandma runs it. I'll go ask her if there are any rooms available there.'

He went up to the counter and spoke quietly to the waitress for a few minutes.

'Done.' He plopped back down in the booth with a sigh of relief. 'She says her grandma's got two rooms at the back of the house. They're not premium, so she hasn't tried to rent them out until she can get them spruced up a bit. I told her maybe I could help out with that. In return for the rent, I mean.' He looked up shyly at Ruth.

'Good job,' she said. 'That'll at least give us some shelter until we can figure out the next move. Now, as to the deed: what we need to do next is find out if there are any taxes owing on the place.'

'Taxes?' He looked stricken. 'I can't pay no taxes, not right now. I'll just have to let it go.'

'Don't be in such a rush to give up on everything. There's always a way out.' She pulled out the deed and spread it out on the table in front of her. 'This is a gift deed made out to you from your grandfather. Now, nobody can take it away from you, but you could lose it if you don't take responsibility for the ownership. That means we're going to have to go down to the Hall of Records, wherever that is for this area, and look up the property as it's described here. Then we'll be able to find out if there's any money owing for taxes. This deed is less than a year old, so you should be okay, unless your grampa hadn't paid the taxes on it for a while.'

Jésus scratched the dark stubble on his jaw. 'I don't know. Gramps didn't have a lot of money. He got Social Security, I think. But I never knew him not to pay a debt he owed. If he owed taxes, I think he would have paid them.'

'Good. Let's hope he did. The taxes on that land out there might not amount to much, since there's not much of a building on it. It looks to me like there's about an acre of land. That's pretty good. You could probably build a pretty nice house there . . . put in some solar energy . . . might not be bad at all.'

'Build a house?' He looked dumbfounded. 'Where would I get the money to do that?'

'You need to get a job. Go back to school if you can. Learn how to do some of the construction yourself. It *is* possible,' she said. 'All you have to do is believe in yourself.'

He sat there silently, staring out at the street. She could tell he was entranced with the whole idea of it. His own place, built with his own hands.

'And if you had someone like Sheri at your side to help you, it wouldn't seem like work at all,' she added.

'Come on,' he said suddenly, rising out of his seat. 'Let's go on down to that rooming house and get set up there. I'll talk to Sheri's grandma about helping out there, at least until I can find a better job.'

'And tomorrow we'll go find out about the taxes,' she said, laying the payment for lunch on the table, including an extra-good tip for the waitress. 'Tomorrow is a new day. Let's hope it brings us both some better luck.'

19

First thing the next morning, Ruth insisted they go to the local post office and rent a box. 'That way,' she said, 'you'll have a permanent address you can give out for employment and anything else you might need it for.'

By the time they got to the registrar's area of the Hall of Records, there wasn't much of a line, so Ruth and Jésus (or Juan, as he was called on the deed), didn't have to wait long to talk to the next available clerk.

'How may I help you?' the woman said, eyeing the two of them suspiciously.

'My nephew here has a deed of gift to real property that was bequeathed to him by his grandfather last year,' Ruth said. 'I'm trying to help him check to see if there are any taxes owing, and to establish a local mailing address for him so he can receive notices in the future.'

The clerk blinked. Most of her

customers didn't have that clear an understanding of the process. Maybe this query wouldn't be so difficult after all.

'Let me just take down the information and run it through our records,' she said more pleasantly. 'I'll be right back.'

As they watched, she scurried back and forth to several file cabinets, pulling out documents and checking with the paper in her hand. A few minutes later, true to her word, she flitted back to her station.

'Here it is,' she said, handing over her notes. 'I can make a copy of it for you if you like. The taxes are all paid up through to the end of the year. The new bills will be going out in December, but next year's payment won't be due until January. At that time, you can either pay the whole amount at once, or you can pay half of it in January and the rest in May.'

'Can you tell us how much the yearly tax will be?' Ruth kept her fingers crossed it wouldn't be anything exorbitant.

'Hmm, let me see. This would only be an estimate, since other factors, like road assessments, might change . . . but right now it looks like the whole year is a little over $375.00. Half would be a little over $188.00 dollars. There's a slight fee for doing it that way.'

'Is there any way we could pay in advance?' Ruth asked. Beside her, Jésus made a little motion of rejection, but she ignored him.

'Well, that's a little unusual,' the clerk said, 'but yes, you can make a payment toward next year's taxes in advance. It'll be figured into the next statement when it's mailed out.'

'Fine,' Ruth said. 'We'll pay $375.00 toward next year's tax assessment on this property. We'll also give you a P.O. box number for mailing purposes.' She pulled a roll of cash from her purse and carefully counted out $375.00 and placed it on the counter.

'I can't . . . ' Jésus began, but Ruth cut him off with a sharp look.

The woman at the counter busied herself for the next few minutes with making several copies of the deed and its existing tax status, producing receipts of the advance payment, and carefully entering the new P.O. box number into their records.

'There,' she said finally. 'I think that takes care of everything.'

'Thank you,' said Ruth. 'I appreciate your patience.'

After all, she reflected, *please* and *thank you* were magic words, and it was none too soon for Jésus to learn that lesson.

Leading him away from the counter, they sat down nearby while Ruth gave him the papers and went over everything with him again. The property belonged to him, and the taxes on it were now paid up for a full year.

All he had to do now was hold on to it.

20

Detective Greenaway took the notes from his meeting with Mrs. Canty and her boarders and headed back into headquarters. The Newton City Police Department was an efficiently run facility staffed with hard-working and competent employees. It didn't take long for the bureaucratic gears to shift into place.

Summoned to the chief's office at half past six that same evening, Greenaway sighed and prepared for a long night of it. He first called his wife to tell her he wouldn't be home for dinner. In fact, he had no idea when he would be home, if ever again. This one felt like it had legs, and he suspected this case would be high-profile and time-consuming, possibly for weeks. His only hope now was that the authorities over in Cathcart would step in and take over jurisdiction in the matter.

If Ruth Moreland was, in reality, Anne

Cromwell, who knew where the investigation might lead. She had obviously been living here in Newton for weeks now; probably had planned in advance to hide out here, from Mrs. Canty's testimony. If the Cromwell woman had come here to escape prosecution for the murder of her husband, Newton was bound to be involved in the investigation, and even perhaps in any forthcoming trial.

No. As near as he could peg it, he was going to have some involvement, like it or not. He might just as well get used to the fact.

'Come in, Hank.' Chief Allen nodded toward one of the chairs in front of his desk. 'I want you to meet someone.'

A lanky man with neatly combed silver-grey hair and bright blue eyes looked over from the seat next to him. 'Howdy,' he said. 'I'm Sheriff Carter from over Cathcart way. I hear you've come up with some interesting news for us.'

He shook hands with the older man and decided he liked him well enough. Maybe the sheriff would be more than happy to take his notes and comments and relieve him of any responsibility with this case.

'Well,' he said, 'I didn't have any idea my little missing person's investigation would turn in to such a big deal.'

Carter pushed a file towards him. 'Here,' he said, 'maybe you'd better take a look at this. And I'd appreciate any comments you might have about this woman. Do you have any pictures of her?'

'No, as a matter of fact, I don't.' It had been one of the things that had convinced him from the start that the lady in question was not a typical missing person.

'I asked several times at the boarding house if any of the people there had seen or taken any photos of her. None of them had. The older lady claimed this woman didn't think she took a good picture and always turned down any requests.'

'And you checked her room thoroughly?'

Greenaway nodded. 'I didn't go through everything with a fine-toothed comb,' he said, 'but I gave it a pretty good once over. I sure didn't notice any photographs or any other personal items like most folks keep around.'

'All right.' Carter looked at Chief Allen. 'We're going to have to go in with a warrant and make a thorough search of her room. I think we've got enough cause to convince a judge of the necessity. You have any objections?'

'None,' said Allen. 'If this is the same woman they're looking for over in Cathcart, we'll do everything to cooperate here.' He picked up the phone and barked a few gruff orders. 'C'mon, guys,' he said, heading toward the door. 'Let's see if we can catch ourselves a suspect.'

21

They went back by the Donut Hole to celebrate. Jésus was in seventh heaven. He couldn't get over the fact that the whole legal procedure had been so easy.

'You really know your stuff,' he said admiringly. 'That lady changed her tune the minute you started talking all that legal talk.'

'Knowledge is power,' she said, smiling at him. 'Remember that. If you want to control your situation, you have to understand it first.'

As she spoke, she wondered if she had followed her own advice during the last month. How smart, really, had it been to run away from the situation, instead of figuring out how to conquer it?

Sheri was smiling, too. She had talked to her grandmother before coming into work, and was so happy, she told them, that they had taken her advice and rented those extra rooms.

'They're not bad rooms, really,' she said. 'They just need a little work to fix them up and make them comfortable. I have some ideas about that. I could help, if you like.'

She was talking directly to Jésus now. He nodded. 'Yeah,' he said. 'It's not going to take too much to do what your granny wants. But if you want to come over tonight, when you get off work, we can take a look and see what it would take. I'll try to save her as much money as I can.'

'Excuse me,' Ruth said. 'I'm going to the ladies room for a minute.' The two were so engrossed in conversation that they hardly noticed when she left the booth and turned to head toward the back of the room.

'Hold it! You there.' A uniformed man pointed at Ruth from the doorway. 'Yes, you!'

She froze in her tracks. The officer approached cautiously, his hand at his hip where she could plainly see the outline of a revolver.

'What . . . ' she started to say.

'Anne Cromwell!'

211

'Yes . . . ' she answered before she thought in time to deny her true identity and claim her alias.

'You are under arrest in connection with the murder of James Peabody.'

She gasped.

'You have the right to remain silent,' he continued, reciting the Miranda Warning. 'Anything you say can and will be used against you in a court of law. You have the right to an attorney. If you cannot afford an attorney, one will be appointed for you. Do you understand?'

She nodded. 'Yes, I understand.'

'Turn around.'

She complied and felt the iron bracelets closing around her wrists.

'Ruth!' Jésus ran toward her but she motioned him away.

'It's all right,' she said. 'Go back to Sheri. Start your new life. Take care of yourself first. You can't help anyone else until you help yourself first.'

A female officer had entered now, patted her down and took possession of her bag. She could see several other patrol cars, lights flashing, pulling into the lot.

They led her out and over to the front squad car. Holding her head down, they pushed her into the back seat and slammed the door. It all felt like a nightmare that was happening to someone else.

As they left the lot, she noticed out of the corner of her eye a heavy-duty pickup parked up near the entrance of the parking lot, well out of the way of the collection of police cars. A familiar-looking man was standing in front of it, arms folded, looking straight at her.

It was Tomás, who had probably doubted her validity from the very beginning of their encounter. He must have seen or heard something, maybe in connection with the bus wreck, to tie his friend's 'Aunt Frances' to the APB from Cathcart. Maybe, she thought suddenly, there had been a substantial reward offered for information leading to her arrest. If so, she hoped it would do him some good.

God knew it wasn't going to help her any.

22

Later that same afternoon, Gail's office door suddenly swung open and Turner Redland stepped inside.

'Gail,' he said. 'Glad you're in. I'm sorry if I'm imposing, but I need to see both you and Connie immediately.'

She motioned to the chair in front of her desk and pushed a speed dial number on her personal phone.

'Connie?' she said a moment later. 'Turner's here and wants to speak to both of us. Do you have a moment?'

'I'll be right there,' was the terse response.

After Connie had joined them, Turner took a piece of paper out of his briefcase and handed it to Gail.

'What's this?' She glanced at it in curiosity.

'It's a document stating that I'm firing you, Connie, the firm, and all your associates, as of today, from representing me or the D.A.'s office in any kind of action, civil or criminal. And I'm going to need an acknowledgment from you, also in writing.'

'All right,' she began. 'And the reason being . . . ?'

'We accept your request,' Connie interrupted her. ' . . . without prejudice. Call Margaret in,' he added to Gail. 'We'll need to draft a recusal.'

She nodded and called in her assistant.

Once Margaret was seated to one side with her notepad at the ready, Gail dictated a brief statement to the effect that the firm of Osterlitz and Brevard and their associates were no longer of counsel to Turner Redland, the Office of the District Attorney, nor to any of their colleagues. The document further noted that the firm had, on this day, received from said Turner Redland written confirmation of that fact.

Margaret left the room to prepare the document for signature, and Gail sat back and waited. 'You owe us an explanation,' she said.

'Easy, Gail,' said Connie. 'I think I

know what this is all about.'

She flicked her eyes to his. 'And that would be . . . ?'

Connie nodded at Turner. 'Be my guest . . . '

He nodded. 'I've just received notification from the sheriff that Anne Cromwell has been arrested by the local authorities in Marshall. They're processing her now and will be conveying her by car down here to Cathcart later on this evening.'

Gail blinked. 'That's great news, but I still don't see — '

'She'll be remanded to the county court here, and will most likely be put forward for arraignment as quickly as possible. Tomorrow morning, if all goes well.'

Gail glanced at Connie, who was nodding vigorously. 'I'm assuming she's asked for a court-appointed defense attorney?' he said.

Everything suddenly flashed into focus for Gail. If Anne Cromwell were charged with the murder of her husband, as it appeared she would be, she would need to be defended in court.

'Yes,' she said. 'I see. Is there anything else you're at liberty to tell us?'

'No,' Turner said. 'I think, under the circumstances, it would be best if I leave now and we probably should not speak further . . . unless, for some reason, this procedure goes differently than we think.'

'I agree,' said Connie, rising. 'Thank you very much, Turner, for bringing this situation to our attention. I'm sorry our firm can no longer be of service to you.'

The two men shook hands.

'And thank *you* very much,' the D.A. said, as he turned to leave. 'I believe we understand each other. I presume I'll be seeing you in court.'

★   ★   ★

Once the caravan of squad cars reached the Marshal police station, Ruth Moreland aka Anne Cromwell was photographed, her fingerprints were taken, and any personal items she had been carrying were bagged and she was given a receipt.

The female officer who had accompanied her from the start was very kind to her, helping her through each and every step of the booking procedure.

Finally, after what seemed an eternity, she was handed a fresh stack of prison apparel and motioned into a private cell to change her clothing. Her street clothes were also inventoried and added to the bag of personal items.

She tried to cooperate with them as much as she could, although she felt violated and frightened. All she could think of was escaping, but she saw no possibility of that now.

Maybe she shouldn't have stayed around to help Jésus/Juan with his personal affairs and troubles. He was very young and would have years to figure out the system and how it all might work in his favor. And maybe she should have just made a run for the border and taken that bus to Los Angeles from Newton, dressed in her older suit-lady role. The story of Jim Peabody's death might not have made as much of a splash in a big urban area like L.A.

What had she been thinking? She continued questioning her decisions, even as they hustled her out of the police facility and into the parking block at the back of the building.

'Here,' said the lady officer, giving her a paper bag as she was handed back into the car. 'There's a sandwich in there. You'll probably get hungry before we take the time to stop. If you need a drink, just holler. I can't leave the bottled water with you, you understand. But I'll see that you get something to drink if you need it.'

'Thank you,' she murmured, tucking the bag down beside her. 'I appreciate your thoughtfulness.'

The woman flashed a warm smile her way. 'You just hold up now, sweetie,' she said. 'Sometimes these things end up not being nearly as bad as you think.'

★   ★   ★

As Turner was leaving Gail's office, a younger man passed him in the hall and gave him a nod. 'Sir,' he said.

'They're waiting,' Turner said, smiling

219

in return. 'I suspect this is going to be a long night for you.'

Damon Powell looked at the older man quizzically. He wondered if the D.A. knew something he didn't.

'Come on in, Damon,' Connie called. 'Join the crowd.'

He took a seat at the conference table, where Gail and Hugo were already deep in conversation. 'What's going on?' he asked. 'Have I missed something?'

'Why don't you start,' Gail said. 'I assume you're here with some information about that matter I was discussing with you.'

'Yes. Marilyn would have come, too, but this is the night she usually gets together with her dad. We wanted to talk further with you about Anne Cromwell and what we found out at the university.'

'Great. That's what I was hoping. But before you start, maybe we should go ahead and tell you the news we just received, which I believe you'll find of interest. Connie?'

'Well,' Connie said, 'I don't know how you'll feel about this. But it very much looks as if we, the firm I mean, may be involved in the Cromwell/Peabody case on the defense end of things.'

'What?' Damon looked from face to face. 'But why? Has something happened?'

'Anne Cromwell was arrested earlier this afternoon in Marshall, of all places,' Gail said. 'By all accounts, she's being transported here to Cathcart as we speak and will appear for arraignment at the County Court House tomorrow morning.'

'But . . . ' Damon said. 'But that means . . . ' He looked from one serious face to the other. 'But I thought we . . . you . . . were representing Turner Redland in connection with this case. Wouldn't that be a conflict of interest? To plead for the defense, I mean?'

'Yes, under normal circumstances,' Gail said. 'But a few short minutes ago, Turner Redland marched in here and fired us, the firm, all of us. We're now free to handle Ms. Cromwell's case, if she so desires.'

Damon sat back in his chair and

thought for a moment. 'I'll need to tell you, then, what Marilyn and I found out about her at the university.'

Hugo pulled a yellow pad towards him and flicked his pen. 'First of all,' he said. 'Who exactly did you speak with at the school?'

'Quite a few folks, actually,' Damon said. 'And everyone we talked to, who had had anything to do with her, remembered her in positive terms.' He fumbled in the briefcase at his side, pulling out a yellow pad of his own. 'Why don't I photocopy our notes for you,' he said, looking at Hugo. 'Then we can go down the list together. Marilyn took most of them, and her handwriting is much more legible than mine. I think most of what you'll need will be right here.'

Margaret was summoned again and took Damon's stack of notes to the photocopier, where she ran off several copies and passed them out to those at the table.

'Yes,' said Hugo, after reviewing his set, 'this is perfect. Some of these people should make good character witnesses.'

Gail nodded. 'Good job, Damon,' she said. 'But now I'd like you to give us a sense of the woman in your own words. What do you really think she was about? Right now, she's almost a complete cipher to us. Can you flesh her out at all?'

23

The squad car hurtled down the highway toward Cathcart as darkness began to descend over the deserted landscape.

Full circle, Anne Cromwell thought. *I've come full circle. And now, in spite of all my efforts to hide away and start over, here I am again, on my way back to the beginning.*

At first, she leaned back and tried to rest, even though her thoughts were a jumble in her head. Gradually, one idea in particular began to gel. What if she could escape again? Could she be smarter about her choices, if she were given another chance?

Finally, after several hours of steady driving, Officer Mark Cleveland, the driver, slowed and pulled off for a gas stop. His cohort, Officer Jane Wickstrom — 'Sweetie' in Anne's mind — came around to the back of the car and motioned their captive out.

'Rest stop,' she announced, guiding their shackled prisoner toward the washroom. After stepping inside and checking the area for possible windows or weapons, the policewoman pulled a set of keys from her waistband. 'Here,' she said. 'I'm going to undo one side of the handcuffs and then I'll step outside to give you a little privacy. I'll have a smoke in the meantime.' Clearly, she did not consider her prisoner to be any risk for escape.

As soon as the door closed, however, Anne began looking for an out. The first thing she noticed was that the outer door had a privacy button lock on the inside, and the overhead light was controlled by a nearby wall switch. Quickly, she pulled up the swinging lid top to the trash barrel parked beside the one sink. She stepped back to one side of the door, flicked off the light switch, and waited, heart pounding.

About five minutes passed before the door slowly swung open and Jane Wickstrom, reeking of cigarette smoke, stuck her head inside. 'What the . . . ?' she got out, just before Anne swung the metal trash bin lid, hard, directly over Wickstrom's head.

The officer's unconscious form crumpled to the floor. Anne pulled her in to the room, shoved the door shut and locked it, then turned on the overhead light.

She bent and checked Sweetie's pulse to make sure there was still a steady heartbeat. Reassured that her victim was still alive and breathing, she grabbed the officer's keys and set about figuring out the locks on the handcuff still clipped to her wrist. In a short time, she had the handcuffs on both of Sweetie's wrists with the linking chain secured behind the sink drainpipe. It wouldn't take long to yank the pipe loose, but the longer Anne had to make her escape, the better.

Next, she pulled off a scarf drawn around the officer's neck, rolled it up tightly, jammed it into her captive's mouth and tied it in place. Again, the officer would eventually be able to pull it out, but it would take a little more time.

Sweetie was still unconscious, but Anne knew she only had a few more minutes of leeway. She pulled Sweetie's tote bag to her and checked the contents. Just as she hoped, there was an extra change of clothes inside.

Her hands flying, Anne stripped off her bright orange prison garb and jammed it in the top of the trash barrel. Sweetie's wallet and change purse went down into the tote, while her revolver was thrust into the toilet water tank.

Dressed in Sweetie's plain black skirt and white tee, a heavy knit grey sweater drawn over the top, Anne took one last look around the tiny space. She hadn't changed her shoes, but the plain black prison slippers were not that obvious, and would have to do.

Turning off the light again, she peeked out the door. The squad car was still sitting in one of the fuel bays unattended. Officer Cleveland was probably paying for the gas and buying snacks and coffee in the lit-up facility next door.

Ruth made her way out and quickly by the big plate glass window. Yes, the officer was still inside, yakking with the proprietor, his back to the door.

Once past the storefront, she ran lightly across the gravel toward a big grey bus idling near the front entrance, an indication it was shortly due to leave.

This was her only chance.

If she could talk her way onto the bus, she might be able to escape to another town. There she could take stock of her chances, change her identity yet again, and hopefully move on to another life.

She knocked on the closed bus door. The driver looked down and reluctantly swung it open. 'Yes, ma'am?' he said.

'Hello,' she said, holding out Sweetie's I.D. 'I'm a police officer on assignment and wondering if there's any possibility of getting a ride to the next town?'

He looked at the ID. closely. The police woman's picture was grainy and faint. Anne smiled at him, hoping she would resemble the younger woman just enough to pass inspection.

'You're in luck, Officer,' he said finally. 'I don't have a full load tonight. I'll have to charge you for the ticket, though.'

'What's your next stop?'

'Cathcart. We should get in around 2:00 a.m.'

Her stomach lurched. Back to Cathcart again. But she had no choice. She couldn't stay here. At least she might have a chance there.

'How much is that?' she asked. 'I think I might have exact change.'

'Just a minute.' He pulled out a well-worn schedule and thumbed through. 'That'll be $19.25 for a one-way from here.'

'Let me see,' she said, hoping against hope that Jane Wickstrom had stuffed enough cash in her wallet to pay for the ticket.

She was in luck. She pulled out a $10 bill, a $5 bill, and a handful of quarters from the change purse. Sweetie probably kept the coins handy for vending machines.

'Here,' she said, handing it all over. He eyed it and nodded.

'That's fine,' he said, stuffing the bills into an envelope and chinking the coins into a half-filled jar stowed next to his seat. 'I think there's still plenty of seats open in the back.'

She made her way down the aisle and found an empty row. Pushing all the way in, she tucked the tote in between her and the window, sat back, and took a deep breath.

Now, she thought, *all I have to do is figure out my next move.*

24

Early the next morning, Damon Powell was at the Cathcart County Court House, making his way into the arraignment holding area.

It was the usual cattle call of orange-suited sleep-deprived prisoners lined up against the railing separating the secured area from the rest of the court room. There were a few defense lawyers leaning against the barrier and speaking earnestly with would-be clients: habitual criminals or ladies of the night with mouthpieces on call, the occasional society maven with a proclivity towards shoplifting, and one or two young men, scions of well-to-do families who had spent a night on the town and ended up in over their heads. Most of them would receive a stern reprimand and a slap on the wrist, and would be released on their own recognizance or that of their attorney.

Damon scanned the line-up, referring frequently to the pictures in his hand. The first was the APB of Anne Cromwell's university I.D. and the second was her more recent mug shot from the Marshall City Jail. No one behind the rail seemed to resemble the lady in question, and he finally made his way over to the bailiff stationed near the front of the room.

'Hi, Burt,' he said, holding out his hand.

'Howdy yourself,' said the grizzled veteran of a thousand courtroom dramas. 'Who're you lookin' for today?'

'I'm here to represent Anne Cromwell. She's supposed to have come in from Marshall last night, but I don't see anyone resembling her. You have anything on her?'

'Oh, *that* one,' Burt said. 'Yeah, she was *supposed* to come in last night, all right, but you'll never guess what happened.'

Damon groaned inwardly. This did not sound promising. 'I suppose you're going to tell me,' he said dryly.

Burt grinned. 'Lady overpowered her guard in the bathroom. Knocked her cold, I hear. Then she escaped the area wearing the officer's civvies and carrying her cash and I.D. I don't think they're quite sure yet just how she got away or where she's gone.'

'You're kidding,' said Damon, shaking his head. 'I guess it'll be back to the drawing board for me, then.'

Burt shook his head in commiseration. 'You never can tell about them quiet ones,' he said. 'Looked like a perfectly nice lady just havin' a streak of bad luck.'

'Thanks, Burt,' Damon said. 'See you later.'

He headed out of the cacophony of human suffering that was the arraignment court and back to the relatively sane law offices of Osterlitz and Brevard.

Have I got news for you, he thought.

25

The big grey bus had pulled into the Cathcart city bus station a little after 2:00 a.m. Cramped and exhausted, Anne Cromwell waited until nearly all the passengers had debarked before climbing down herself and making her way into the terminal.

Even at this hour, the room was loud and busy with passengers coming and going, and friends and family either seeing them off or waiting for them to return. It reeked of stale fast food, smoke — in spite of the 'No Smoking' policy widely proclaimed throughout — and unwashed bodies.

Anne's stomach rumbled queasily as she headed toward the lavatory. Once she had completed her ablutions, brushed her hair and added a touch of lipstick from Sweetie's stash in the tote, however, she felt a little more alert and tried to think rationally about what she should do next.

She would be on the current wanted list, that she knew, and perhaps with the ominous 'armed and dangerous' warning as well, if they had not yet discovered Sweetie's pistol in the toilet tank.

Her advantage was that she looked pretty average, with no obvious identifying birthmarks or unusual features. The disadvantage was that many people in this town knew her, from her years of employment at the university and from just being in and about the area for a long time. How you hid from that, she did not know. But she would have to give it a try. She had one little ace in the hole, though. And now she thought how best to use it. It would require a bit of finesse, and even more luck, but she would have to give it a try.

One of her colleagues at the university had become a friend and confidante as well. They were close in the sense that they had spent time together, sharing a meal occasionally, and chatting often about various events in their backgrounds and lives.

This friend, Laurel, owned a small

bungalow in a secluded residential area away from downtown Cathcart. She also knew that the woman had made plans to go out of town to her family's home for an extended vacation, and would be away during much of the time she herself had arranged to be on leave in order to cover her tracks.

With any luck, Laurel had already left the area, leaving her little home vacant and unattended. During previous years, Anne had sometimes looked in on the place during Laurel's vacations, mainly to check on her cat. But the cat had crossed the rainbow bridge a few years ago. Ever since, Laurel had rejected the idea of a regular house-sitter.

'Who would be interested in my old place and stuff?' she had said, grinning. 'I don't have anything of any particular value there. If someone wants to break in and rob me blind, they're welcome to whatever they find!'

Now, in Anne's time of need, she found she still remembered the 4-digit password to Laurel's ancient alarm system; and she knew for a fact that the house key probably still resided under a flower pot full of geraniums on the front porch. The problem remained, how was she to get all the way out to the place, especially in the dark. It must be at least five miles from the bus depot. She didn't dare hire a taxi or try to take a city bus through town, and it would be insane to show her face on the city streets.

The only solution, as she saw it, was to strike out walking, sticking to the back streets as best she could, and hope she still had enough energy left to make one more trek. She thought long and hard about the house's location and which streets to use before gritting her teeth and heading out the front entrance and onto the darkened thoroughfare.

This was not Main Street, but it was only one block east of it and a little to the north of the downtown area where more lights were showing. She would need to go south one or two blocks, then head west on the least busy, and darkest, side streets she could find. She hefted Sweetie's tote bag up to her shoulder, turned to her left, and headed out with determination.

Oh, how she longed to toss the nasty reminder of what she had done to that poor woman into the nearest trash bin. But she knew if the bag was discovered and identified, the authorities would know immediately that Anne Cromwell had landed in Cathcart. And she was determined to avoid that possibility as long as she possibly could.

She tried to set an even pace, not striding exactly; she was far too spent for that. But she figured if she kept walking steadily for as long as possible, she would at least be closer to her destination before dawn. Plus, the further away from the downtown area she could get, the more likely it was that no one would recognize and report her to the police.

At least that was what she hoped.

★　★　★

By the time she was approximately halfway to Laurel's house, she was completely exhausted. She stopped in the middle of the block she was currently traversing and wavered, suddenly unsure.

I will not pass out, she ordered herself. *Just stop and get your breath. You're almost there. You can't give up yet.*

Then she spied it, just off to her right. Sitting back away from the street was a small bit of cleared land. It was surrounded by bushes and a few trees, flowering perhaps, although it was hard to tell in the dark. A lone street light revealed a central cement monument of some sort. And adjacent to the statuary reclined a single park bench, empty and deserted in the moonlight.

She heaved a sigh of relief and struggled over to it, stumbling through the grassy lawn and dragging the tote along behind her by one loose strap. Arriving at the bench, she leaned back, gazing up at the stars sparkling here and there in the velvety night sky. Here she could catch her breath and replenish her strength for the last leg of her journey. It felt like salvation.

She rested there for what seemed to her to be a very short time, but was probably longer than she thought. Eventually, the sky began to lighten a bit toward the east. She had no idea of the time, but dawn was on its way. It was time to get on the move again.

She stretched and rose from the bench cautiously. Her leg muscles were still aching; her feet, still encased in the inadequate prison slippers, were sore; and her head was throbbing. Still, everything seemed to be working, and as she stepped out through the little park and back on to the street, she felt confidant she could finish the journey without incident.

This area of town was much less densely populated, and the further she went towards the west, the fewer houses she passed. There were more trees, and the undergrowth was denser here. The sidewalks disappeared and the road narrowed. No traffic had passed her for the last mile or so.

She marched along, determined to keep up her current pace, and she was still hauling the derelict tote bag by its one strap. Her journey seemed endless now, and she had the feeling she would spend the rest of her life placing one slipper-clad foot in front of the other. Sometimes she counted aloud, 'One, two, three . . . ' up to ten or twenty before starting over again, just to keep motivated and make the time pass.

The morning sun was just beginning to show itself above the treetops when she suddenly stopped short and took a deep breath.

There it was!

Laurel's quaint little bungalow sat just ahead of her, on the opposite side of the street. It was less than a block away, and she was so moved by the sight of it that a few tears squeezed from her eyes and slid down her pale cheeks. Breaking into a half run, she flew across the street, the tote bag banging along behind, and ran up and onto the tiny front porch. Her hands shaking so she could scarcely control them, she reached down to move the terracotta pot sitting next to the door, hoping against hope that Laurel had not changed her setup since the last time she had been here.

Yes! There it was, just as she remembered, cradled in the hollow holding the pot. She grabbed her prize, straightened to pull open the creaky screen door, and carefully fit the slender brass key into its matching lock. It resisted a bit but finally gave way, allowing her to turn the handle and open the door. An immediate beep-beep-beep erupted from a panel on the wall just inside the tiny entryway. She quickly examined it and punched in a short series of numbers as she remembered them. The beeping stopped and the little red light turned to green. She was in luck. The password still worked.

She looked behind her into the street. There were no houses nearby, no pedestrians, and no cars traveling in the street. She might have been on the moon, the area seemed so deserted. She swung both doors shut, locking them behind her, and left the tote bag in the corner of the entry. There would be time enough to deal with it later.

A quick survey of the kitchen revealed that the utilities were still connected, and there were a few items in the tiny refrigerator and its freezer compartment that would supply a meal or two. The heat also seemed to be on at a very low setting, probably to keep the pipes from freezing. She would be able to stay warm without resorting to the fireplace.

She turned her attention to Laurel's bedroom. It was connected to a tiny bath, and the hot water was working. She stripped, dropping all of Sweetie's clothing she had been wearing into a corner of the room for disposal with the tote.

Cranking up the hot water, she climbed into the shower and shampooed her hair and scrubbed her body, standing under the steamy stream until she felt clean again. Once she had toweled dry, she put on soft flannel pajamas she found in a drawer and returned to the bedroom.

Without any hesitation, Anne Cromwell climbed into her friend Laurel's queen-sized bed, piled high with soft pillows and warm quilts, and fell into a deep, dreamless sleep, the best she'd had in some time.

Anne slept most of the morning away. In fact, she was so deeply asleep that she never noticed when there was a commotion in the driveway outside, followed by the clunk of footsteps on the front porch and, finally, the click of a key in the door.

The bedroom door swung open, the drapes were flung aside, and bright sun streamed in on the bed.

'What in the world!' The woman standing there was looking down at Anne as if she'd seen a ghost. 'What are *you* doing here?' she continued. 'How in the world did you get in?'

Anne stirred. At first she reacted with shock and fear, but then when she realized who was standing there and what had just happened, she sat up. 'I'm so sorry, Laurel,' she said, her voice still raspy with sleep. 'I'm so very sorry I've done this to you. But I didn't think I had an option.'

'Hmm,' said the other woman, taking a seat in a small rocker in the corner of the room. 'Do you feel like talking about it?'

'I suppose I'm going to have to tell you. Everything, I mean. That is, if you don't already know.'

'All right,' Laurel said. 'Why don't you take your time, get up, get dressed and come on out to the kitchen. I'll fix us something to eat, make some coffee. Then we can sit down and hash it over. Obviously, there's *something* going on that I haven't heard about yet.'

'Well, if you haven't, you're probably the only one in the world who hasn't,' Anne said. 'Did you just get back from your trip? I thought you'd be gone longer.' She pushed back the quilt and sat up, testing her muscles, and groaned a bit. 'Whew,' she added. 'I think I could use that breakfast and coffee. Do you have a robe or something I could borrow? Then I'll tell you everything you want to know, and probably a whole lot more.'

A while later, the two women were seated across from each other in a cozy breakfast nook, finishing Laurel's hastily prepared breakfast and sipping cups of hot black coffee.

'So,' Laurel said, 'you not only are wanted for murdering poor old Jim in cold blood, you're also on the run for knocking out a policewoman and stealing her money and identity. What could possibly go wrong with all that?' She snickered a bit, then put on a more serious face. 'Sorry, Anne,' she said. 'But everything you've told me so far is so fantastic as to be unbelievable. How in God's name did you get yourself into such a mess?'

'I don't know, Laurel,' Anne replied. 'I honestly can't tell you. Except every step of the way I thought I was just getting out of a situation which had become more and more unbearable. You know, I sincerely didn't wish Jim any ill. I just wanted to get away from him. I thought if I could do it in such a way that he'd still have use of the money for a while, that it would make up for me abandoning him like that.'

'Well,' Laurel said dryly, 'you certainly didn't make things any easier for yourself in the process.'

The two women sat there a moment in silence, both lost in their own thoughts. Finally, Anne stirred. 'I realize now that I have no choice, really. I don't know what I thought I was doing, breaking into your home like this. I know it was a complete invasion of your privacy, not to mention a breach of our friendship. I don't think I can ever — '

'Stop it,' said Laurel. 'I don't want you to say another word about it. You're my friend. If I can't open my home to you, then I don't deserve to be called a friend. You'd do the same for me, in a heartbeat, of that I'm certain.'

Anne began to cry then, in earnest, tears streaming down her face and plunking into her coffee cup.

'There, there, honey,' said Laurel. 'You have a good cry and get it all out. Then we're going to sit down and figure out what to do next.'

26

'Where in the world could she be?'

Gail stopped her pacing in front of her office window overlooking Main Street and turned to the others in the room.

'Where on earth could she have gone in the middle of the night, without much in the way of resources, and everybody in the world looking for her?'

'Your guess is as good as anyone's.' Hugo shrugged and sat down his cup of coffee, the third one he'd had that morning.

'She's either very resourceful, or she's had a lot of good luck to have escaped scot-free for this long. I just hope she hasn't come to harm somehow. The longer she's out there on her own, the more likely it is she'll run up against something she won't be able to handle.'

Connie was poring over all the notes he'd put together, trying to match up what they already knew with all the different stories they'd now acquired from the various authorities involved, from the Marshall City Police Department to the Cathcart County Sheriff's Office, Sam Weems's office notes, and even a few clandestine memos from Turner Redland and his sources. None of it seemed to make much sense. A mild-mannered female university professor, middle-aged and with no known criminal background, had suddenly gone off on a rampage across the state involving several different identity changes and a possible assault against a police officer, and she also just happened to be the leading suspect in her husband's murder.

'My best guess is that she somehow managed to escape from the washroom at the rest stop without attracting any attention. Question is, how?'

Hugo thought a moment. 'Maybe she had an accomplice,' he said. 'After all, we know she'd made at least a few friends in each of the places she's known to have stayed before she was arrested.'

'Yes,' said Gail. 'According to Detective Greenaway's account, the people at that

249

boarding house in Newton were all very supportive of her. He said they couldn't believe that she'd done anything wrong, let alone murder her husband.'

'And that kid in Marshall — Juan or whatever his name is,' Hugo added. 'He had nothing but good things to say about her when they got around to questioning him. He said the lady was actually helping him turn his life around.' He scratched his head and took another sip of coffee. 'All of those people seem to believe she's Mother Teresa or something.'

'There is *one* good thing about all that,' Gail said. 'It might make it a little easier to mount a defense for her. At least we should be able to come up with some character witnesses on her behalf.'

'There is that,' Connie agreed. 'If we can actually find her so we *can* defend her.'

Just then, Damon Powell's phone buzzed. 'Excuse me,' he said, and stepped away from the desk to take the call. A moment later he called out: 'Guess what!'

'Please tell us you've got some good news for a change,' said Gail.

'I don't know if it's good or bad,' he said, 'but that was Burt, the bailiff over at the arraignment court. It appears that Ms. Cromwell has surfaced and contacted the local authorities. Apparently she's been in touch with a friend who's talked some sense into her. The two of them are coming in together to the police station sometime tomorrow morning.'

Connie turned to Hugo. 'Put some feelers out and see what you can find out about this friend and what he or she might have to do with the case. And Damon,' he added, 'you should be at the police station the very first thing tomorrow. We need to make damned sure Anne Cromwell knows she has someone ready to represent her.'

27

The next morning, bright and early, Anne Cromwell and her friend Laurel Johnson ate a light breakfast and headed out to the main police station in downtown Cathcart. The two women were of a similar size and build, so Laurel had produced a plainly tailored pantsuit and low-heeled dress shoes that fit Anne well enough.

They ran Sweetie's skirt and top through the light cycle of Laurel's washer-dryer. Then they carefully folded the clothing, added Sweetie's wallet and I.D., and laid them all down into the tote bag. Laurel even tucked an additional twenty-dollar bill into the change purse so none of Sweetie's money would be missing.

'I don't know why we're doing this,' said Anne, brushing as much of the mud and debris off the tote as she could. 'They're still going to be accusing me of assaulting a police officer.'

'It's the best we can do to fix the problem,' said Laurel. 'If it looks like you've tried to return her things in as good a shape as possible, maybe they won't go so hard on you.'

Anne shrugged. The police assault was the least of her worries. She had no idea how she was going to defend herself from the accusation of killing Jim Peabody. Not after running and disguising herself the way she had.

Finally, Laurel looked at her watch. 'Nine a.m.,' she said. 'It's time to go.'

She picked up the tote and motioned Anne ahead of her to the door and out to the driveway. Laurel's old compact car stood waiting, and the two climbed inside. She started the engine, and off they went.

Anne watched the scenery pass by as if in a trance. Only a day ago, she had struggled to walk this distance from town. Now they were whizzing down the country road in a matter of minutes. Almost before they knew it, Laurel was slowing to pull into the municipal lot next to the police station.

'Looks like they're pretty full,' she commented, circling through the lot. 'Tell you what. Why don't I drop you off in front of the steps there? You can wait until I find a parking spot. It shouldn't take me too long. Then we can go in together.'

'You don't need to do this, Laurel,' Anne said, mouth trembling. 'You've already done so much for me. I'll never be able to repay you as it is. Why don't I just say goodbye now and go in on my own. You can leave, and I won't even mention your name. No sense in dragging you into this mess.'

'Nonsense!' Laurel reached over and patted Anne's knee. 'I haven't had anything this interesting happen to me in years, if ever. There's no way I'm not going to see how all this turns out. No, you just wait right here for me. I won't be five minutes. Then we'll go in together, just as we planned.'

So saying, she handed out the tote bag to Anne and began circling the lot again, watching for the next available parking slot. Anne stood watching Laurel's car going up and down the rows, wavering

254

between the temptation to walk on into the station on her own and the equally appealing notion of having some moral support as she surrendered herself to the police.

'Good morning!'

She started, and looked up in the direction of the familiar-sounding male voice. Her face turned pale and chalky, her vision blurred, and she suddenly felt as if she were about to faint dead away right there on the sidewalk.

'No!' she said, choking on the bile rising in her throat. 'No! It can't be!'

★ ★ ★

By the time Laurel parked her car on the far side of the lot and walked the 100 or so feet back to the police station entrance, Anne Cromwell had disappeared.

At first, Laurel was disappointed. *She's done another runner*, she thought. *She was too afraid*. Then she had an even darker thought.

What if Anne *had* killed Jim? Maybe she actually was a murderer trying to escape justice. If so, she, Laurel, had been made a fool. But she thought she knew Anne's character better than that. She had probably gone on inside and turned herself in, choosing to leave Laurel out of it entirely.

She looked down. The tote bag was still sitting on the pavement next to the tarmac. Either Anne had forgotten to take it with her . . . or she had deliberately left it behind. Either way, Laurel knew she was out of her depth. Turning resolutely, she made her way up the steps and into the lobby of police headquarters.

'May I help you?' said the sergeant on duty.

'I hope so,' Laurel Johnson said. 'I certainly hope you can.'

28

Damon Powell, as promised, had been at police station headquarters earlier that morning. He didn't wait around outside on the off chance he might spot Anne Cromwell, though. Instead, he went on in and spoke with the sergeant on duty, who confirmed that they had been alerted to be on the watch for a wanted suspect who might come in for questioning.

Damon found a seat and reviewed his paperwork about the case. Every time the door opened he looked up, hoping to see their prospective client. Each time he was disappointed until, at about half past nine, the door opened again and a woman of about the same age and build as Cromwell stepped through the door and made her way directly up to the sergeant's desk.

Damon was close enough to overhear her query about 'Anne Cromwell' and immediately jumped to his feet. 'Hello, ma'am,' he said politely, once the sergeant had confirmed that they had not heard from Ms. Cromwell yet that morning.

'Yes?' Laurel said, turning toward him. 'Do you know what's happened to her?'

This response caught him off guard. 'No,' he said. 'I'm here hoping to speak with her. I represent a law firm that's prepared to offer her *pro bono* assistance, if she desires or needs it.'

'Oh,' she said. 'Well, I just brought her in and left her out front while I parked. By the time I got back to the entrance she was gone, leaving this.' She gestured to Sweetie's tote bag at her feet. 'I have no idea where she's gone or why,' Laurel added. 'The plan was for her to surrender herself to the authorities this morning. I assume you know what her case entails?' she added.

He nodded. 'Yes. We're fully aware of the details of her case. So she was out front while you parked?' he added. 'And now she's disappeared, leaving her bag behind?'

'Yes,' Laurel said. 'I'm very worried

about her. It isn't like her to have done this.'

Damon turned back to the sergeant. 'I may be out of line here,' he said, 'but I'm beginning to think something's happened to her.'

The sergeant was already punching a call button. He spoke earnestly into the intercom before turning back to Damon. 'You two need to stay here. My superior will want to talk with both of you. If something has happened to the suspect right here in front of the police station, we'll need to get to the bottom of it as quickly as possible.'

Damon took out his cell phone and called Gail. He explained what had happened and asked for instructions.

'Stay right there,' she said. We'll try to figure out what to do next.'

The detective in charge had emerged from his inner sanctum and was questioning Laurel. 'What do you mean, she just disappeared?' he said. 'You were right there. How could you lose sight of her?'

'I was looking for a parking spot,' Laurel said somewhat impatiently. 'Shouldn't you be out looking for her? She may have taken ill and moved where she could sit. She's not a young woman, as you must know, and she's been under a terrible strain over the past few days.'

But while they were still speaking to the detective, the front door to the police station swung open again and a stream of people entered, including reporters, Sheriff Carter and his men, and last but not least, none other than District Attorney Turner Redland.

'How in God's name could you let this happen?' the D.A. said to the detective. 'She was right here, and you let her get away. Why in the world didn't you have someone, any live body, on duty here at the front of the building?'

'I thought we did,' the man said, concern creeping into his voice. He was quickly becoming aware of the seriousness of this sticky situation which had occurred right here on his watch. 'I mean, that's the usual policy whenever we're expecting someone to surrender. There should have been a whole team of people watching all of the entrances, not just here at the front.'

'So what happened then?' interrupted the sheriff, shouldering his way past a couple of the reporters blocking the entry. 'Where is this 'team of people' now?'

'Hello, Turner,' a new voice interrupted the chaos. 'Sorry to see you under these circumstances.' The speaker was Police Chief Randall Hobbes. 'Come on back to the office. You, too, Carter. I may have some answers for you.'

Damon Powell moved up. 'Hello, sir,' he said, offering his hand. 'I'm here representing Osterlitz and Brevard. We're prepared to act as defense counsel for the accused. I was set to meet her here this morning, before this all happened.' He gestured in the general direction of the crowded entrance.

'All right,' conceded Hobbes. 'You come along, too.'

The police chief was well aware of the law firm. They might be of assistance in this situation, or at least provide additional information.

The small group followed the chief back to his offices. Chairs were pulled out and once everyone was seated, Hobbes spoke again.

'I do have information about the whereabouts of Ms. Cromwell, which I think you'll all agree needs to be kept under wraps until we have better control of the situation. Carter,' he said, addressing the sheriff directly, 'you may have heard some of this already, just through channels, but I'm going to bring these other gentlemen up to date as well. Is that all right with you?'

Sheriff Carter nodded. 'That seems fair. Go on, Randy. You'd better let them know what we know. No point in keeping it all to ourselves.'

★ ★ ★

A short while later, Damon Powell and Turner Redland left the station to head back to their respective bases.

'I think it goes without saying,' Turner said as they turned toward the car park, 'we both are going to be putting in a very long night.'

Damon nodded soberly. 'I'm just

wondering, sir . . . '

'If you have any concerns at all, young man,' the D.A. said, ' . . . we have not had this conversation.'

And with that, he fled the scene of the crime — leaving Damon to work it all out for himself.

29

'Order, order in the court!' Bailiff Burt Holmby stood demanding attention near the front of the room. 'All rise. Court is now in session. Judge Balcom presiding.'

Voir dire had been completed a few hours earlier, and following lunch, the hastily empaneled jury and their alternates had been reassembled in the box assigned to them. The judge entered, gathered his black robes, and took his place at the dais.

'Be seated,' Burt spoke again.

There was a general shuffling and scraping as the participants settled in for the opening phase of the hearing. Once things had quieted down sufficiently, the bailiff approached the bench.

'Good morning, your honor. First case on the docket is the People vs. Cromwell. Both parties are present.' He laid a packet of papers in front of the judge.

Balcom took a few minutes to review

them, although it was a certainty he already had perused every piece of paper pertaining to this case in great detail before entering the courtroom. 'Thank you, Burt,' he said. He looked out over the room before riveting his gaze on the accused. 'Ms. Cromwell,' he said, not unkindly, 'before we begin, do you feel you have adequate representation?'

Anne nodded. 'Yes, sir,' she said.

Her voice was so low the judge had to bend nearer to hear her. His eyes flicked over to the three other individuals seated at the table. Connie rose to address the court.

'Yes, your honor. Conrad Osterlitz here, if you please. I'm speaking for the firm of Brevard & Osterlitz, with the assistance of Damon Powell of Watson & Powell.'

The judge nodded. 'Very well, Counselor. It shall be so noted for the record.' He turned his attention to the prosecution. 'And I see that the district attorney himself is on hand to represent the people in this particular matter.'

Turner Redland stood. 'Yes, your

honor. The people stand ready.'

'Very well.' He waited as the court stenographer completed her entries. 'Bailiff,' he intoned, 'we shall now proceed with the trial at hand.' He glanced down at his notes again. 'I understand some new evidence has emerged regarding this particular case,' he added. 'I'm hoping that opening statements from both parties will help clarify the matter for all of us, but most specifically for the jury. Are there any objections or preliminary comments from either side at this juncture?'

'No, your honor,' said Connie. 'None as yet for the defense.'

'No, your honor. The people are prepared to proceed also,' Turner echoed.

'Good. Let's hear from the prosecution first, then. Proceed when ready, Mr. Redland.'

Turner Redland rose, walked to the podium, and looked down at his prepared notes. At his table, several assistants were already bundling additional papers preparatory to provide the D.A. with anything else he might need as he worked his way through the opening statement.

He took a sip of water and cleared his throat. 'Your honor, ladies and gentlemen of the jury, and my fellow counselors and colleagues,' he said, bowing toward the defense table, 'we have before us here today a fascinating tale of murder, mayhem, and malice the like of which this town has seldom seen.'

Interestingly, the defense table didn't stir at this revelation, but seemed as riveted to the D.A.'s words as the spectators in the gallery were.

Anne Cromwell was huddled between Gail and Damon Powell. At Gail's insistence, she had been allowed to attend in street clothing and would be unshackled throughout the trial. She sat silent and poised, as if none of the D.A.'s words pertained to her at all.

Redland continued with his narrative. 'Now James Peabody, by all accounts, was something of a con artist and a gambler; someone who was always scheming to make money the easy way, by scamming innocent victims of their hard-earned cash. In other words, he was a no-good lowlife; someone who'd never done a lick of clean, honest work for a day in his life . . . a person most folks would cross the street to avoid.'

He paused and glanced over at the still figure at the defense table.

'On the other hand, here we have his wife, Anne Cromwell. She's well-educated and employed as a respected professor at our university here, and to all who know her, she seems to be a quiet, decent, hard-working individual of impeccable reputation. But inexplicably, on the day in question, Ms. Cromwell walked away from her home, her job, and her husband with nothing but the clothes on her back. She left all of her personal effects behind and fled to a remote city, where she took on a completely new identity and began a new life.

'Ladies and gentlemen, I think you'll agree that her behavior in itself is suspicious. But even more ominous, it's obvious from what we later discovered that Ms. Cromwell had planned this entire disappearing act months in advance. Yes,' he continued, 'this mild-mannered woman had, long before she ever set foot out that door, established a completely new identity, secured a place of residence, and — even more telling — siphoned away thousands of dollars from the bank accounts she held in common with her husband without his knowledge or agreement!'

There was a stirring in the gallery. Redland had the spectators in thrall.

'So, what are we to believe when a day or two after the lady had gone through her vanishing act, her husband, James Peabody, was discovered, a victim of cold-blooded murder, in the den of his own home — the home he'd shared up until that very moment with his wife, Anne Cromwell?'

At this point, Redland turned directly toward the defense table and stared meaningfully at the woman seated there.

'I am not going proceed any further with this discourse, your honor,' he said, bowing toward the bench. 'But I shall now leave it in the hands of defense counsel to explain, if they are able, just why it is that Anne Cromwell fled the scene of her husband's cruel murder after planning her escape so precisely, and so well in advance.'

'Thank you, Mr. Redland,' Judge Balcom said. He seemed puzzled and a bit disappointed that the prosecution had cut its opening statement so short, but it was, after all, their choice. He looked over at the defense table. 'Are you ready to proceed?'

'Yes. Thank you, your honor. Defense opening will be delivered by Ms. Brevard.'

Gail rose and took her place at the stand. 'Your honor,' she said. 'Ladies and gentlemen of the jury. Colleagues.' She nodded toward the prosecuting team. 'I'd like to take you back to the evening in question when Anne Cromwell chose to give up everything she owned and treasured.

'First, she left her career at the university, a place where she was admired and respected by all who knew her, and she also walked away from the home she'd paid for with her own earnings. Not only that, she left at least half of her financial assets for her husband's use, and she abandoned a community where she was well-known and had valued friendships. Why would she do this? What possible motivation could she have had to make such a drastic change in her living circumstances?

'To answer that question, we must go back to her relationship with the man she'd married and lived with for a number of years, James Peabody. She knew from the very beginning of their relationship that he was not anywhere near her equal in intellectual terms. But by the time they met, she was middle-aged, somewhat of a recluse, and, even more importantly, Anne Cromwell had begun to consider herself to be past a 'marriageable' age.

'James was personable, easy-going, and, as Anne tells it, 'he could always make me laugh.' She understood that he saw her more as a meal ticket than in a romantic way. But in her view, his somewhat questionable companionship seemed better than facing a solitary old age.

'And so they were married. They quickly settled into a daily routine which consisted of her university work, while Jim had the freedom and money to follow whatever pursuits he fancied. They did spend time at home together, more or less compatibly, and enjoyed the occasional evening out.

'At some point, however, several years in to the marriage, Anne Cromwell began to notice a critical change in her husband's personality. The happy-go-lucky Jim Peabody of earlier years suddenly developed a mean streak. He began cursing and picking arguments with her, something he hadn't done before. Even more sinisterly, he began threatening her physical well-being. People at the university noticed her increasing absences, and a few of her closest colleagues began to spy cuts and bruises which she found difficult to hide or explain away.

'We now are prepared to document, in fact, that the James Peabody of this period developed a reputation amongst his other cohorts for a bad temper and outright violence. In one case in particular, a woman with whom he had dealings was badly injured, and we will provide documentation that he was the responsible party.

'Now, some clarification of the happenings on the particular evening Anne Cromwell made her getaway. She recalls being drawn into a violent argument with James Peabody, one in which he threatened her very life. And she states that she had no doubt at that time he meant what he said.

'In her view, she had no choice. Fearing that this very scenario might be a possibility, she had made plans in the several months prior to this final altercation to leave Cathcart and start her life over in a new place. And that's precisely what she did.

'She insists, however, that on the evening in question, she left the man she knew as James Peabody in the den of their home, alive and well. Several days later, when the news of his murder broke in Newton, the town where she'd set up her new residence, she fled that area in a panic. She admits that some of the choices she made were not good ones. But she's adamant that she did not kill her husband . . . nor did she ever conspire to do so.

'Ladies and gentlemen of the jury, Anne Cromwell is an innocent woman and a victim of mistaken identity. And we're prepared to prove this fact to you beyond a shadow of doubt.' Gail paused for effect, nodded at the judge and Turner, and took her seat.

There was stunned silence in the courtroom. Balcom pondered his notes for a few more moments.

'Chambers . . . everyone,' he said abruptly, rising from the bench and making his way back to his private quarters. The bailiff instructed the jury to await further instructions and motioned to both the prosecution and defense counsels to follow the judge.

Anne stayed where she was, a jail matron hovering watchfully nearby. She glanced back at the company behind her and drew in her breath. Marilyn Powell, Damon's wife, was seated immediately behind the defense table, as was Laurel Johnson beside her. That was no surprise. The two women had helped her dress that morning. Mari Powell had combed her hair for her.

But what shocked her so much were the faces staring back at her from the next row behind Mari and Laurel. Mrs. Canty, resplendent in her Sunday-go-to-meeting outfit with the matching pearl necklace and earrings which her husband had given her on the occasion of their last wedding anniversary, was seated next to the aisle. When she caught Anne's eye, she blew her a kiss. Lined up in the row next to her were Dumb Dora, Bill, Joe, and Jack. All smiled at her, and Jack waved shyly. Dora gave her a quick thumbs-up.

Several people she didn't know came next. But there, two rows immediately behind her, sat Sheri and Juan. Sheri was dressed in a neat cotton dress and wiggled a finger at Anne. Juan was nearly unrecognizable. He was clad in a neat navy-blue suit, white shirt and striped tie. His longish hair had been trimmed and was slicked back, and he was clean-shaven. He no more resembled the punky Jésus of Anne's first acquaintance than the man in the moon.

Anne smiled, for the first time in what seemed like forever, and waved back at all of them.

However else this crazy situation played out for her, at least she had made a few friends along the way, and that had to be a positive thing.

30

After what seemed like an eternity, Judge Balcom, followed by the various attorneys and their assistants, made their ways back out into the buzzing courtroom.

'All rise,' intoned Burt again. He waited until everyone had returned to their respected places before announcing: 'Be seated. Court is now back in session.'

The jury members, who had been hoping for some kind of a break, settled back down grumpily.

'All right,' Balcom said. 'Here's what's going to happen now.' He nodded to the stenographer, who sat poised and waiting for his next instructions. 'I'm going to terminate these proceedings for today.'

The jurors all smiled. But there was some grumbling from the spectators, who had expected more of a blockbuster announcement.

'The jury is hereby excused with all of the usual admonitions and prohibitions on your conduct still in place until this trial has been declared completed. That means you must not discuss this case or any subject connected with the trial amongst yourselves or others, including family members, the bailiff, the attorneys and other officers of the court, or even to reporters who may ask you questions or for your opinions. Nor may you read anything about the case at hand in the newspapers or watch accounts of it on television or the internet. Furthermore, you all will report back to the jury room tomorrow morning at 9:00 a.m. precisely. Is that understood?'

The foreman stood. 'Yes, your honor. I believe everyone here understands the rules.'

'Fine,' the judge said. 'You're excused.'

As the jury filed out, he turned his attention back to the bailiff. 'I'm adjourning for today only. We'll take up deliberations first thing tomorrow morning. Any questions?' he directed toward the D.A. and Connie.

'No, your honor,' both men responded in unison.

'Fine. See you here tomorrow, then. Hopefully we can conclude this thing successfully at that time.' So saying, he stepped down from the bench and retreated to his inner sanctum.

Court was over for the day.

★ ★ ★

Anne stepped out of the tepid shower and into the terrycloth robe handed to her by the ever-present attendant. *It's a good thing I'm not royalty*, she thought. *I could never get used to having someone always next to me, handing me things and shepherding me from my room to the shower and back. Of course, there's still no certainty I won't be doomed to doing this for the rest of my life.*

On that sober note, she reviewed all that had happened over the past few days. The very worst part of it had been those first few moments at the police station when she thought for sure she had finally lost her mind. Later on, when everything had been revealed to her, she was more than a little angry about it all, especially when she reflected on how she had been used — and not just by Peabody. The authorities had not come off too well in this fiasco, either.

But now at least she had a fighting chance at a reprieve, if only her trial would be resolved as she hoped.

Tonight she remained in captivity. Tomorrow would tell the tale.

31

'Hear ye, hear ye,' called out Bailiff Burt. 'The court of the Honorable Judge Balcom is now in session. All rise.'

The courtroom accommodated Burt and the magistrate took his place.

'Be seated,' Burt added, almost as an afterthought.

Judge Balcom looked out over his domain. 'Ladies and gentlemen of the jury,' he said, 'the new evidence I spoke of at the beginning of this trial has now been confirmed for me by the District Attorney's Office, the County Sheriff's Office, and numerous other organizations and individuals who have come forward to testify on Ms. Cromwell's behest. Because this information is overwhelming in its conclusions, I'm prepared at this juncture to entertain a motion by the district attorney, speaking on behalf of the People, to dismiss all homicide charges against Ms. Cromwell pertaining to the murder of the individual known to this community as James Peabody, aka Jim Peabody.'

The response from the jurors and spectators in the courtroom was overwhelming, especially from the second row back, where all Anne's supporters were gathered. Mrs. Canty's boarders were all smiling and waving at the defendant. Juan had actually jumped up out of his seat and unleashed a celebratory fist pump before Sheri tugged him back down. Laurel Johnson and Marilyn Powell hugged each other, their friendship now sealed in joy.

Judge Balcom sat back and motioned to the bailiff to let the celebration continue for a minute or two, before gaveling everyone to attention.

'We're not through here,' he said. 'I will now ask District Attorney Turner Redland to proceed with his summary of this case and his motion to dismiss. I assume there are no objections from the defense?'

'None, your honor,' Connie responded quickly.

'Very well, Mr. Redland. Please proceed.'

'Yes, your honor.' Redland stood at the podium and glanced over at Anne Cromwell. 'Ladies and gentlemen, I'm not here to delve any further into the background of Ms. Cromwell's decision to leave her husband at the particular time she chose, nor is there any need to rehash her change of identity, her choice of items to take or leave behind, or any of her other decisions to hide from the authorities. I believe her defense team has explained all of that thoroughly.

'Suffice it to say, she did not always make the wisest of choices — but I don't believe her primary goal, ever, was to defraud anyone. What I do believe is that she was terrified throughout much of her journey, and trying only to escape detection and capture. That, in and of itself, I submit, is *not* a crime. Nor, in my opinion, does she deserve to be penalized or punished further for the terror and hardship she's already endured.'

He paused and took a sip of water before continuing. His audience was fully attentive now. You could hear a pin drop in the silent courtroom.

'I'll pick up my narrative at the point in time when Anne Cromwell was discovered back here in Cathcart by a close friend who took pity on her and gave her shelter. Ms. Cromwell confided all that had happened to this person, who was then able to persuade her it was time to surrender to the local police.

'The defendant agreed and called in her plan to turn herself in at our local police station the following morning. When the two arrived, they discovered that the parking lot was nearly full. The friend dropped Ms. Cromwell off at the entrance to the building and drove on to locate a vacant parking space. What happened then is so bizarre — and so unthinkable — that it begs credibility.'

The audience sighed in unison. They felt as if they were watching a thriller on TV and were eager for the next installment.

'Somehow the news of Ms. Cromwell's time and place of surrender got leaked to the wrong parties. When she and her friend arrived at the station that morning, trouble was waiting. As she stood on the sidewalk while her friend parked the car, she was approached by an individual who greeted her, taking her by surprise. Imagine her shock and consternation when she realized she was looking into the face of none other than James Peabody, her husband, and the man she'd been accused of murdering.'

The courtroom erupted in earnest, and the bailiff stood and called out for there to be 'silence and order in the court' or people would have to leave.

As soon as things were quiet again, Redland continued his story. 'I'm not going to belabor you with unnecessary information that won't move us forward,' he said. 'But of course you must know the truth of the matter, which is that Anne Cromwell and James Peabody were married. Mr. Peabody had been described as an amiable sort, none too reliable, but harmless. Ms. Cromwell was seeking companionship, and Mr. Peabody enjoyed being supported financially. Their relationship proceeded successfully on that basis for a number of years. What we, and Ms. Cromwell, did *not* know was that James Peabody was an identical twin.'

There was a gasp from the spectators, but they kept quiet, wanting to hear more.

'The twin, Joseph Peabody, resided in a small rural community upstate with their father, Jerome Peabody. James had never confided this fact to his wife — but his father and brother did know about her.

'At some point, Joe Peabody got greedy. He decided that Anne Cromwell was too much of a good thing to be wasted on his more easy-going twin. It didn't take long for Joe and his father to hatch a scheme so nefarious that it defies the imagination to outline it . . . but I must.

'Periodically, and without Anne's knowledge, James Peabody visited his father and brother. We believe he shared some of his wife's money with them on these occasions, and also bragged about the easy life he was leading with her help. During one of these visits, Joseph

Peabody, angry and jealous, imprisoned his brother in the family house under the watchful eye of their father. Then Joseph Peabody, under the guise of his twin brother James, returned to Cathcart, where he took his place as Anne Cromwell's husband.

'But Joseph was not the same man as James. He had a cruel and violent nature. Petty crimes and misdemeanors became outright theft, assault, and even blackmail. And the first person to notice the difference, of course, was the one closest to him, his wife. By the time she made her final decision to disguise herself and leave the area, she was frightened for her life

'Ironically, it was on this very evening that the real James Peabody had finally overpowered his father. Breaking free of his bondage, he made his way back to Cathcart, intent on regaining his life and home. When James arrived on the scene, he confronted his brother in the den. The fight which ensued must have been desperate. Joseph contends that the gun with which he had threatened Anne's life earlier in the evening went off of its own accord, and that the fatal shooting of his brother was either an accident or undertaken in self-defense.

'In any case, James Peabody ended up dead of a gunshot wound in the home he'd once shared with his wife, Anne Cromwell. Joseph Peabody made his getaway and returned to his father's home upstate.' He paused and shook his head. 'It was Cain and Abel, a tale as old as time itself. Brothers so conflicted that it resulted in fratricide. No one was the wiser, and the only person who seemed to have had both motive and opportunity was Anne, who hadn't helped herself by running away from the scene just hours earlier.

'Now, we're near the end of our tale,' Redland said, 'so please bear with me. When Joseph Peabody confronted Anne Cromwell at the police station, she of course was horrified. The man in front of her was by all intents and purposes her husband, James Peabody, who was supposed to be dead.

'What Joe Peabody didn't know, however, was that the police department had staked out the entire perimeter of the station. They wanted to be absolutely certain of taking Ms. Cromwell into custody safely and without incident. Joe Peabody probably intended to kidnap Anne Cromwell and do who knows what with her. But he didn't have a chance. He was surrounded by deputies before he could make a move. Joseph Peabody was arrested and subsequently charged by my office with the murder of James Peabody, and will be brought to trial as quickly as the court sees fit. Thank you, your honor,' he said, and returned to his seat.

Everyone sat stunned, except for the principals, and even they showed signs of shock. Judge Balcom gaveled for attention.

'One might think,' he said, 'that we'd now adjourn and this case would be closed. But there's one other piece of business we still need to address. And that's why I've asked you, members of the jury, to remain empaneled.'

The jurors looked at each other in disbelief.

'During Ms. Cromwell's mad dash to escape the authorities and remain free, there's one event we can't overlook. In accordance with the APB having to do with the Peabody murder, she was captured, placed under arrest in Marshall, and subsequently put in a squad car under police guard to be returned to Cathcart. Halfway through the journey, she's accused of overcoming her female attendant at a rest stop and escaping, once again. Still pending against Ms. Cromwell, therefore, is a charge of assault against a police officer. And that, ladies and gentlemen of the jury, is the final matter we must conclude here today. Mr. Redland, are you prepared to present the people's case against the defendant in this matter?'

'Yes, your honor.'

'Is the defense prepared to act for the defendant in this case?'

'Yes, your honor,' answered Connie.

'Very well, we may proceed.'

Turner Redland got up again and outlined the relevant facts pertaining to the assault of Officer Jane Wickstrom, which were reputed to have taken place in the washroom of a rest stop located halfway between Marshall and Cathcart. He was succinct and did not belabor the details.

Balcom motioned to the defense. 'We concede the overall details as outlined by the district attorney,' said Gail.

'Very well,' said Balcom. 'The people may call their first witness.'

'The people call Officer Jane Wickstrom,' responded Redland.

Wickstrom was sworn, took her place in the witness stand, and gave her name and rank.

'Thank you,' Redland said. 'Do you now recognize in this courtroom the defendant, Anne Cromwell?'

'Yes, sir,' the witness replied. 'She's the lady sitting at the defense table.'

'Good. Now, on the evening in question, can you, in your own words, describe for us what transpired in the washroom at the rest stop?'

Sweetie flicked a glance toward Anne and nodded. 'Yes, sir,' she said. 'We'd stopped, as scheduled, for a gas and food break. Following protocol, I entered the washroom first and checked it for any possible escape exits or weapons. I unlocked one of the bracelets of the defendant's handcuffs, leaving one of her hands free. I then stepped outside to allow her a few minutes of privacy.'

'What happened next?'

'When enough time had passed, I opened the door to reenter the washroom. I was surprised to find that the overhead light was out and the room was in total darkness.'

'What did you do?'

Sweetie grimaced. 'Well, I'm embarrassed to tell you that I stepped into the darkened room without thinking. Somehow I caught my toe on a mat next to the door and fell face forward onto the floor. Knocked myself cold, I did, and I have no idea how long I was out.'

There was stunned silence in the courtroom as the judge, jury, D.A. and, most of all, Anne Cromwell digested what the policewoman had just said under oath.

'Hmm.' Turner Redland looked down

at his notes in puzzlement. 'Er, are you saying, then — '

'I'm saying that I fell forward into the room, hit my head, probably on the tile floor, and lost consciousness. By the time I recovered, Ms. Cromwell was gone. I have no idea where she went from there, or what might have happened to her after that.'

'And what happened to *your* personal belongings, Officer? Do you know if the defendant took or used them? Were they ever returned to you?'

'Oh, yes,' Sweetie said. 'All my things were left in very good order. So far as I could tell, nothing had been used, and all my money and identification were still right where they should have been.'

The D.A. glanced over at the defense table. Gail and Connie looked straight ahead, not daring to move. Anne Cromwell was staring at the witness in shock.

'No further questions,' Redland said at last. 'Your witness, Counselor.'

'Your honor,' Gail said, rising to take the podium, 'the defense has no questions for this witness, and in light of her testimony, we'd like to put forth a motion to dismiss on the basis there is no evidence to substantiate the charge of assault on a police officer.'

'The people have no objection,' Redland added, almost too quickly.

'Very well,' Judge Balcom said. 'In view of the testimony we've just heard, and unless there are any other witnesses?' He glanced at Turner and Gail, who both shook their heads rapidly. 'In view of all that, your motion to dismiss is granted, Ms. Brevard. This trial is hereby concluded. The jury is also dismissed and the defendant is free to go.'

A cheer went up throughout the entire chamber. Even the jurors chimed in.

Anne's friends from the second row descended on her, offering congratulations and assistance with whatever direction her new life would take.

'You must come visit us whenever you can,' Mrs. Canty was saying. 'I won't hear different. I'm keeping your room for you, and you can stay there as long as you like.'

Juan Bautista, the young man who had saved her from the bus wreck, broke in with a big grin. 'And we're planning on getting married soon, Sheri and me,' he said. 'We're just waiting 'til you can come to the wedding. Her granny's looking forward to seeing you again, too.'

Marilyn Powell and Laurel Johnson had already suggested a celebratory lunch for the three of them the following day, mainly to discuss their plans to push for Anne's immediate reinstatement at the university.

'But I want you to stay with me tonight, at least,' Laurel added. 'Then we'll take a look at that house of yours; make sure everything's clean and sparkling before you start staying there again.'

Watching them, Gail reflected that all of Anne's troubles had begun because she was so afraid to be alone. Now, after the trauma she'd been put through, all the friendship and love she'd been seeking for years was flowing in her direction.

'Why do you think she did it?' Connie

said, watching Officer Wickstrom leave the courtroom.

'Commit perjury, you mean?' Gail said as she packed up their files, ready to head back to the office. 'I have no idea. Maybe she really *didn't* remember exactly what had happened to her in that darkened washroom. When she heard the atrocities Anne had endured, and saw all the support for her in the courtroom, even from the jury, I believe she became willing to give her prisoner the benefit of the doubt. That's what always surprises me about the law,' Gail added. 'It seems so rigid and even predictable. But every once in a while a kind of rough justice emerges, influenced, perhaps, by unplanned acts of social consciousness. And in my opinion, that's exactly what Sweetie has performed here today — an act of random kindness.'

She glanced over at the prosecutor's table. Chief Hobbes and Sheriff Carter were huddled deep in conversation with Turner Redland. She hoped that reason would prevail and that Officer Jane

Wickstrom would receive nothing more than a slap on the wrist and a brief leave of absence before being allowed to return to her duties without further penalty.

One thing Gail was certain of: Turner Redland had no intention of pursuing any further charges against the officer in connection with this case. He was already looking ahead to the trial and conviction of Joseph Peabody for the murder of his brother in the first degree.

Joe Peabody would need defending, of course, and she couldn't help but wonder who would end up with that disagreeable assignment. She shook off the thought for now. But she knew it would remain, lurking like a silent spider in the cobwebs of her mind, until the question came up again, likely in the near future.

Connie and Gail celebrated their victory briefly with Hugo and Damon, then left the office and headed out to the old Norris house, where Cousin Lucy and Erle awaited them with a hot meal and celebrations of their own.

It would feel good to get back into a normal routine again, for however long that might be. And Anne Cromwell, seated amongst her new friends and smiling at them all through her tears, was seeing justice through a slightly different lens.

'Do to others as you would have them do to you,' had been her mantra. And she had tried to follow that principle as best she could throughout her ordeal.

It was not always an easy path, she reflected, counting her blessings. But in the end, what harm can it ever do to be kind to others?

We do hope that you have enjoyed reading this large print book.

Did you know that all of our titles are available for purchase?

We publish a wide range of high quality large print books including:
Romances, Mysteries, Classics
General Fiction
Non Fiction and Westerns

Special interest titles available in large print are:
The Little Oxford Dictionary
Music Book, Song Book
Hymn Book, Service Book

Also available from us courtesy of Oxford University Press:
Young Readers' Dictionary
(large print edition)
Young Readers' Thesaurus
(large print edition)

For further information or a free brochure, please contact us at:
Ulverscroft Large Print Books Ltd.,
The Green, Bradgate Road, Anstey,
Leicester, LE7 7FU, England.
Tel: (00 44) **0116 236 4325**
Fax: (00 44) **0116 234 0205**

ON THE WORST DAY
OF CHRISTMAS

Tracey Walsh

When Bethany's childhood sweetheart Jake signs up to attend Chatham Hill School's Christmas reunion, she follows suit, despite her misgivings about returning to the eerie building. Arriving at the old school, Bethany notices something unusual about the reunion organiser — she looks considerably younger than she'd sounded over the phone. As the snow falls thicker, a disturbing fact becomes clear: only a few of the Class of '96 have not been told that the reunion is cancelled. Little do they know that even fewer of them will be allowed to leave . . .

MURDER AT CASTLE COVE

Charlotte McFall

Librarian Laurie decides that a literary festival is just what Castle Cove needs, but it becomes clear that not everyone with an interest in the town agrees. As the festival gets underway, so do several sinister occurrences: threatening letters, missing manuscripts — and murder . . . When disreputable crime writer Suzie is sent to the festival, she resolves to blend into the background. But after she bumps into an old adversary and meets a new friend, she is sucked into the centre of a real mystery — one that she is determined to solve.

GROWING LIGHT

Marta Randall

Who wanted George Ashby dead? Who didn't? Anne Munro is thrilled to land a job at Growing Light, a New Age software company in rural California. But the company's lax atmosphere veils an unconventional cast who have only one thing in common: they hate George Ashby, their control-freak leader. Ashby soon gives Anne reason to hate him, too. After the discovery of his corpse, she must prove that wielding a knife is not a skill she left off her résumé — and clear her name by finding the real culprit.

FIND THE MONEY

Tony Gleeson

The mysterious Vanessa has vanished, and it's worth a million dollars to a vicious drug lord to get her back. But the ransom disappears, turning up in the hands of a bewildered innocent bystander, while ruthless gangsters and hapless kidnappers alike desperately search for the money. Meanwhile, Detective Marlon Morrison, who only wants to comfortably ride out the final year and a half before his retirement without incident, finds himself involved with a growing succession of murder victims, and a bizarre case growing in complexity by the hour . . .

DECEPTION

V. J. Banis

Playboy Danton Rhodes preys on rich women, squandering their fortunes before the inevitable divorce. He never expected to fall in love with Lois Carter, a married woman with a watertight prenuptial agreement; but when he learns that Lois's stepdaughter Dee needs to marry before her next birthday in order to receive her inheritance, Danton smells an opportunity. As Dee's cousin Helen arrives at the family home, she finds chaos — Lois has been violently attacked, and the suspect is none other than the familiar face she picked up along the way . . .